SWIPE RIGHT TO BITE

NEW ORLEANS
NOCTURNES

CARRIE PULKINEN

Swipe Right to Bite

Contact Information: www.CarriePulkinen.com

Cover Art by Rebecca Poole of Dreams2Media

ISBN: 978-1-957253-00-8
First Edition, 2021

Dating a demon is pure hell…

Succubus Katrina is fasting for her freedom. If she can ignore her demonic urges long enough, Satan will eventually forget about her, and she'll be free.

Just because she isn't getting it on doesn't mean she can't help the supes of New Orleans do the pants-off dance-off.

Introducing Swipe Right to Bite, the best and only hook-up app for the supernatural. Business booms from day one, and the horizontal tango becomes the most popular dance in the Big Easy.

Until Gabe, the insufferable incubus, shows up and ruins everything.

There isn't enough room in this town for two fornicating fiends, and Katrina is determined to send this guy packing, no matter how hot a fire he lights in her nether regions.

But Gabe has a few tricks up his sleeve, and he won't make it easy on her. The question is, how hard will she make it on him?

If you like sassy heroines and hot-as-sin demons, you'll love this fast, funny paranormal romantic comedy!

CHAPTER ONE

"Satan's balls on a silver platter." Katrina Alarie stopped in the shade of a nineteenth-century two-story and refreshed the page on her phone. "This has to be a glitch."

"What's wrong?" Jasmine, her necromancer BFF, wiped a bead of sweat from her forehead. The late afternoon sun hadn't sunk far enough behind the buildings to provide relief from the sweltering heat, but Katrina didn't notice.

She ground her teeth and hit refresh again. "C'mon, you sorry piece of Cerberus shit."

"Holy hellhounds; that's some big shit." Jasmine laughed. "Come inside. I'm melting out here." She gripped Katrina's arm and tugged her into The Tipsy Leprechaun, a bar for supes on Frenchman Street. "They have the most glorious AC. Sit. Talk."

One good thing about being born in the bowels of hell…New Orleans' hot and humid weather didn't faze a demon. Katrina slid into a seat at the bar and turned off her phone. Maybe a reboot would fix the glitch.

Colorful bottles containing every liquor known to

man—including a few potions reserved for supes only—lined the shelves behind the counter, and a small stage across the room stood empty, a jukebox filling the air with music as they waited for the band to arrive.

"Good afternoon, ladies." The bartender, a warlock with dark hair and colorful tattoos, grinned as he approached. "What can I get for you?"

"Abita Amber, please," Jasmine said.

"Whiskey neat." Katrina held the man's gaze, and his jaw fell slack. "Please." She turned her phone on and stared at the screen, willing the damn thing to hurry up and start already.

Jasmine leaned toward her and whispered, "Your demon is showing."

"Christ on a cracker. Shoo. Go get our drinks." She made a go-away motion with her hand, and the man blinked, returning to his senses.

Inhaling deeply, she reined in her succubus magic. Demons never revealed their powers, though Katrina's were hard to hide. She wasn't a shapeshifter, but when her demon was showing, she looked like the hottest exotic dancer to grace the most upscale strip club with her presence. And not one of the opening acts either. She'd be the main attraction.

She *was* the main attraction back in the day. Having the power to turn men—and women—into drooling idiots by simply being in the room with them made stripping a lucrative business. It was fun for a while, but it was also way too tempting. Katrina was a succubus, for Satan's sake.

She. Loved. Sex.

But she was fasting for her freedom. Under Satan's command, she was supposed to ruin men. Break up marriages. Poison their minds. And she did for quite a while. She was the Devil's favorite succubus…in more ways than one. In fact, the reason she was even allowed to live topside was that she was banned from hell when the idiot's girlfriend caught him with his head between Katrina's legs.

After spending one hundred fifty years with humans, she'd grown fond of them, and she no longer wished to ruin them. She was a succubus with a conscience. Go figure.

But she had the urges ingrained in her psyche. Sex with humans—or supes—could still ruin them, whether she wanted it to or not, so she abstained as much as possible. Sure, she had a slip up every decade or so, but she didn't do it on purpose.

She wanted to be out from under Satan's rule, and as long as she stayed celibate, the Devil would forget about her eventually. Once he did, she'd be free. The urges to destroy men would cease, and she could live a normal life. Other demons had won their freedom. Why not her?

Returning to her soccer mom guise, she took a long sip of whiskey, closing her eyes and focusing on the gentle burn cascading down her throat. "Mmm… That's better."

Her phone's home screen finally lit up, and she opened the back end of Swipe Right to Bite, her online dating app, which she'd used most of her life savings to build. If she couldn't get this glitch fixed, she'd be out a shit-ton of cash. "Fuck me with a jackhammer!"

"Are you going to tell me what's up, or should I guess?" Jasmine asked.

"Thirty-two men canceled their subscriptions in one day. In *one* day!" She closed the app and turned her phone over on the counter. "Why would they do that?"

Jasmine sipped her beer, looking thoughtful. "Not enough hot women on the app?"

"No, that's not it. All the filters are included with their subscriptions. Hell's bells, they don't even have to make an effort. The app will put makeup on them, shave someone or even give them a beard. It'll crop out their boring backgrounds and put them on the beach. There is no excuse for looking average on my app."

"Maybe that's the problem. They're expecting to meet a ten, but a four shows up to their date."

Katrina scoffed. "If people are stupid enough to think everyone looks as good in person as they do on social media, they deserve disappointment."

Jasmine lifted her hands. "I'm just saying, there's more to relationships than looking good."

"It's a hook-up app, Jazz. People don't use it to find relationships; they use it to get laid."

It was the perfect setup for a fasting succubus. If she couldn't enjoy her own romps between the sheets, at least she could help others have a little fun. Sex was therapeutic. It relieved stress, it made people release all kinds of feel-good hormones, and her app enabled supes who weren't in relationships to fill their need for intimacy, no strings attached.

If a hook-up turned into something more, good for them. If it didn't, no harm done. This was the twenty-first century. It was time to shatter the Puritan stigma that sex was bad.

Katrina had spent most of her existence destroying people. Now she could atone for her sins and help people learn to enjoy the act for what it was. A mutual good time...emphasis on the mutual.

"Let me send a quick email to my app developer, and

then I promise we'll have our girl time." Fighting the urge to write in all caps, she asked Antoine to include a second *Are you sure?* screen when someone tried to deactivate their account, warning them all their potential matches would be gone forever if they canceled. Maybe a little FOMO would help with client retention.

"There." She slipped her phone into her purse. "How are things in reaper land? You're drinking beer, so I assume it's not happening in the baby Death department?"

Jasmine laughed. "We're taking a few years for ourselves before we start adding to the reaper population. Now that I don't age, we have all the time in the world."

"Lucky you." Katrina smiled as a tall, dark, and delicious gator shifter approached the bar to order a drink. "Well… Hello, handsome." She shouldn't have, but she couldn't help herself. The man was scrumptious, and she let her guise slip ever so slightly, just enough to catch his attention.

His eyes glazed for a moment before he blinked and flashed a cocky grin. "Hey there, beautiful. Can I buy you a drink?" He sidled up right next to her and brushed a finger over the back of her hand. If he wasn't currently under the influence of succubus magic, that would have been a creepy move. She could forgive him though. He truly couldn't help himself around her.

Jasmine cleared her throat. "I thought you were trying to win your freedom."

Katrina gave her the stink eye before turning to the shifter. *Mmm…* She could screw him six ways to Sunday, make him forget his own name, and enjoy every delectable second of it. But Jasmine was right. Annoying, but right.

"Thanks, hon, but I can buy my own drinks." She winked, breaking her spell, and turned toward her friend.

"Bitch," the shifter grumbled.

Katrina straightened, ready to tell the alphahole off, but Jasmine caught her arm and shook her head as Crocodile Dundee skulked away with his drink.

"How dare he? Just because a woman declines a man's drink offer, it does *not* mean she's a bitch. It means *she has taste*." She shouted the last part over her shoulder, but Gator Dick was already across the room.

"And just because you're a succubus, it doesn't mean you should put every attractive man you meet under your spell."

"I wasn't going to *do* anything with him. You have no idea how difficult it is to be this fabulous and not flaunt it. It's nice to know I've still got it." And one day, she'd be able to *use* it without destroying the object of her affections.

"You said you're *fasting* for your freedom."

"Yeah?"

"Fasting means no snacks."

She pursed her lips and glared at her friend. "It was just a little nibble."

"And nibbles lead to bites, which lead to full-blown meals."

"I have it under control."

"Says every addict."

"Oh, fine. I'll behave." Her friend was annoyingly right *again*. No demon truly had their magical urges under control, not even the ones who'd won their freedom. It was why those who lived topside with the mortals were required to attend weekly Hellions Anonymous meetings.

Katrina, of all demons, should know how easy it was for a hellion to slip. She was the coordinator of the New Orleans HA chapter. And, okay. Yes, she'd slipped a time or seven. It happened. That was one of the reasons she started her dating app. She could do what she loved from a distance.

"Thanks for keeping me in check." She polished off her whiskey and tapped the bar to get the warlock's attention. "Another round, please."

"That's what friends are for," Jasmine said.

A band took to the small stage and started their set with an Ed Sheeran cover. Not a bad choice. Katrina did have a thing for the pasty ginger type. To be honest, she had a thing for all types, but whatever.

Though it was daylight outside, the club owners had painted all the windows black, and shaded lights cast a smoky haze over the bar. The door on Frenchman Street was always locked, the actual entrance to The Tipsy Leprechaun hidden in the alley.

Most of the human world didn't know supes existed. The higher-ups in government and law enforcement knew, which was why Hellions Anonymous was a thing, but they held their knowledge in the strictest confidence. Humans would shit a brick if they knew actual demons…and vampires and shifters…lived among them.

"Looks like we weren't the only ones with Tuesday Happy Hour on the brain." Crimson, the high priestess of the New Orleans witch coven, sashayed toward them. Her black hair spiraled down to her shoulders, and winged eyeliner accented her dark brown eyes.

"Hey, Jasmine. Hi, Katrina." Sophie, a red wolf shifter with blonde hair and blue eyes, smiled at them before flagging down the bartender and ordering drinks. "Have you met the new demon in town? I hear he's a hottie."

Katrina straightened, giving Sophie her full attention. "No, I have not. Tell me more." Demons were required to register with her and attend HA meetings as part of their treaty with the humans. They all knew that. So this guy was either avoiding or just passing through, and Satan help her, he'd better be just passing through. Otherwise, she'd have to hunt him down, which would be such a pain.

"He's staying at Gaston's B and B. I think he's running some sort of counseling retreat or lecture series or something."

"What kind of counseling?" And what in hell's name could a demon help people with? They were all rotten to their cores, no matter how nice they tried to be.

Sophie puffed her cheeks as she blew out a breath. "I'd have to ask Jane. She's the one who told me about him, but I wanna say it had something to do with relationships or intimacy or something. His name is Gabe if that helps."

"Are you talking about the emotional intimacy lectures?" The bartender set their drinks on the counter—a glass of chardonnay for Sophie and a vodka sour for Crimson.

"That's what it was. Thank you." Sophie grabbed her wine and took a sip.

"He stopped by last weekend and dropped off some flyers. Here." He grabbed one from the end of the bar and handed it to Katrina.

"Son of a bloodsucker." Her mouth fell open as she read the page.

Mastering Emotional Intimacy with Gabriel Dakota.
Get off the dating apps and focus on finding true love.

"Get off the apps? This fucking fiend is here to ruin me!" Her blood boiled, her anger making her soccer mom guise dissolve faster than a sugar cube in absinthe. "He found me. Shit! He found me."

"Katrina." Crimson put her hand on Katrina's wrist, and calming magic tingled across her skin, reminding her to breathe.

She cracked her neck and glanced toward the dance floor where people were grinding on each other in groups of three and four. If she didn't get herself under control, the entire club would turn into a giant orgy. Not that it wouldn't be a fun time for all, but still… "Hit me with your magic again, Crim."

Crimson held both her hands and whispered a spell that reduced her panicky anger to ash. "Are you okay now?"

Katrina swept her gaze across the room. People were scratching their heads and looking confused as all get-out, but the sexual energy had died down to a simmer. "Yes. Thanks for that. It's hard to keep my demon in check when my anger gets away from me."

"Who found you, hon?" Sophie asked.

"Satan, of course. And he sent this…this *Gabriel* to torment me. Fucking demons named after angels. That always spells trouble."

"Hey now." Crimson's brow edged toward her hairline. Her husband was a demon named Mike…AKA Michael. "I found a good one."

"Yes, you did." She spiked her voice with sarcasm. "And he didn't cause you any trouble at all, did he?"

Crimson narrowed her eyes. "I see your point."

Sophie slid onto the stool next to her. "I thought all

the demons who lived topside had won their freedom from the Devil."

"Most of them have, but I'm in hiding. Succubi don't have a twenty-four-seven magical connection to Satan like other demons do, so I took a chance after I was banished to New York and came here. He's left me alone for the past century, so I figured he didn't know where I was. Apparently, he found me."

"Maybe not," Jasmine said. "Maybe Gabriel is a recovering demon who's trying to atone for his sins like you are."

"Pshh. Not likely. He's one of Satan's minions here to make my life on Earth a living hell so I'll come crawling back. Well, it's not going to happen." She hopped off her stool and marched to the end of the bar to swipe the rest of the flyers. No way in all of Satan's realm was she going to allow this nonsense to be advertised. And it was *utter* nonsense.

"Look at this," she said as she returned to her seat. "He says you should learn to be intimate without sex. How ridiculous is that? Sexual intimacy is the *only kind* of intimacy. Satan's off his rocker. Nobody's going to fall for this."

And yet they had, hadn't they? This so-called lecture series was the only explanation as to why so many men would cancel their accounts on her app. Not to mention the mass exodus happened right after his all-male class yesterday evening.

Sophie's lips puckered. "You've never been in love before, have you?"

Katrina forced a dry laugh. "Succubi under Satan's control can't fall in love. Neither can incubi for that matter. We're *sex* demons. We don't have the capacity for romantic love."

"Hmm…" Jasmine tilted her head. "Can't fall in love? Or choose not to?"

"Well, I've never heard of one falling in love." And she couldn't begin to fathom what it would feel like. Her range of emotions was limited to horny, satiated, pleased, and mad as hell.

She arranged the flyers, tapping them on the bar to even out the stack. "There's no sex demon manual, but the idea of monogamy sounds so foreign to me, I can't imagine it being possible." She'd like it to be. Her friends seemed to enjoy it, but as long as Satan held her under his thumb, it wouldn't be happening for her.

Jasmine shrugged. "Yeah, well, most reapers aren't capable of falling in love, yet I happened to find one who was."

"If it's possible, I am not one of them, and that's not even the point. The point is that Satan sent this man here to ruin me, and I'm not going to let that happen." Gripping the flyers in both hands, she ripped them in half, restacked them, and tore them in two again. Yay for demon strength.

"What are you going to do?" Crimson asked.

Katrina held up a shredded piece of the flyer and pointed to the date. "I'm going to ruin him first."

CHAPTER TWO

Gabe Dakota sat in the living room of the Bellevue Manor Bed and Breakfast, chatting with the owner, a vampire named Gaston. "It's a simple concept. Modern people put way too much emphasis on sex. I teach them to put emotional intimacy first. That's the only way to find real love."

Gaston's dark brows furrowed over ice-blue eyes. "What if your client deems himself unworthy of love?"

"Everyone is worthy of love."

The vampire's gaze grew distant for a moment before he retrieved his glass of blood from the coffee table and took a sip. "Why did you choose New Orleans for this experiment?"

Gabe rested his elbow on the arm of the midnight blue sofa. It wasn't an experiment. His retreats had changed countless lives. "You've got the highest concentration of supes in one place in all of the US. I've been counseling humans for a while now, and I figured what better place to try my hand with the supernatural than the city so many call home."

Gaston touched the tip of his tongue to a fang, his expression skeptical. "What kind of demon did you say you were again?"

"I didn't. Demons—"

"Never reveal their magic. Yes, yes. I'm dirty old. You don't need to explain things to me."

Gabe laughed. "Do you mean 'old as dirt?'"

The vampire ignored his question. "Forgive my mistrust, but I can't imagine a demon dedicating his life and his freedom to helping people. Especially humans."

Imagine his level of mistrust if he found out Gabe wasn't just a demon teaching people sex wasn't important but that he was a recovering incubus. If Gaston knew what he'd been through, he would understand, but that was a story Gabe never shared with anyone. Hell, he didn't even like to recall the memories himself. The constant reminder in his pants was enough.

"It's about as believable as a centuries-dead vampire running a B and B."

"Touché." Gaston lifted his drink in a toast. "It's a back toss to my adult years as a human."

"A throwback?"

"I worked in hospitality before I was turned, and I rather enjoyed it." He glanced at the light-tight rotating door before it spun. "My dinner party has arrived. If you'll excuse me." As Gaston rose, the door turned, and a pair of vampires Gabe had met earlier in the week entered the room.

"Oh, hey, Gabe!" Jane, a brunette with dark brown eyes, said. "How's it hanging?"

He chuckled. If she only knew. "Not bad. It's good to see you again. Hey, Ethan."

Jane's husband nodded a hello. "How was the first session?"

"It was interesting. I had about thirty-five men show up. All kinds of supes. It took some convincing, but I think I got through to a few. Turns out there's a hook-up app for New Orleans supes that most of them were on. I encouraged them to delete their accounts and try meeting people in real life. Not sure if any of them went for it though."

"It's a popular service for those of us not looking for love," Gaston said.

Gabe shook his head. Gaston was one person who would greatly benefit from attending his sessions. He'd even offered him free admittance, but the vampire had declined. "You don't have to go *looking* for love. If you're open to it, and you're not distracting yourself with shallow sex, it will find you."

"We better get going, boys," Jane said. "I have to be at work in an hour, and I'm famished. Nobody wants to see what happens when this much fabulous gets hangry."

"No," Ethan laughed. "No, they don't. See you around, Gabe."

The vampires left, and Gabe picked up a photography book from the end table. It was filled with colorful photos of famous New Orleans landmarks and images from Mardi Gras and all the various festivals the city hosted. He could see why so many supes lived here. It had a rich history, with buildings dating back to the eighteenth century, which was considered almost ancient by US standards.

Of course, Gabe had been around a lot longer than the three-hundredish years New Orleans had been a city. Twice as long, maybe. He'd lost count.

He returned the book to the table and stood. There was no sense in looking at pictures when he could experience the city for himself. He passed through the light-tight door and tapped his key card to a panel, unlocking the exit. Warm, humid air engulfed him as he stepped onto the porch of the nineteenth-century Garden District mansion.

Gorgeous Victorian, Colonial, and Classic Revival homes lined the streets, and massive oak trees shaded their pristinely manicured yards. It was quiet here. Peaceful. But if Gabe wanted to see what he was up against for tomorrow's session, he needed to make like The Little Mermaid and go where the people were. Specifically, the supes.

His host had informed him of two places to observe them. Nocturnal New Orleans was Jane's vampire bar, where vamps went to feed and humans went to be the meal. Of course, the humans thought it was all an elaborate game and the vamps were people wearing fake fangs. They couldn't be more wrong. But thanks to the vampire laws about how often a human could serve as a meal—and the vamps' glamour—it was perfectly safe.

Nocturnal New Orleans wasn't on Gabe's agenda tonight. He was headed for Frenchman Street. He could've easily portaled there, arriving at his destination in a blink, but he preferred to experience the sights and sounds of the city. A streetcar line a block over ran all the way to the French Quarter, so he hopped on New Orleans' most famous mode of transportation and sat on a wooden bench. Of course, they called them trolleys back home in San Francisco, but not here. He'd made that mistake earlier this week and was quickly corrected—it's *A Streetcar Named Desire,* not a trolley.

Gabe, of all people, knew a thing or two about

desire... Hey, he might have been recovering, but he was still an incubus. Always would be. Satan made sure of that.

Fucking Satan. A growl rumbled in his chest as he stepped off the streetcar onto Canal. Long, determined strides carried him across the multilane thoroughfare separating the French Quarter from the American side of the city. As he reached Bourbon Street, a group of women stopped and stared. A man's mouth opened, and his partner's eyes widened.

Gabe's demon was showing, but he didn't care. Every time his thoughts drifted to what that bastard from hell had done to him, anger ignited in his soul, making it nearly impossible to control his magic. On this section of New Orleans' most famous street, it didn't matter. Every other building held a strip club on the ground floor, and Gabe passing through with his incubus powers flowing would get passersby horny enough to forget their inhibitions and go inside.

Satan's balls. What was he doing? Inhaling deeply, he reeled in his magic, morphing from Gabriel, the hottest model to grace the cover of a romance novel, into Gabe, regular guy and emotional intimacy counselor. He had to keep himself in check or he'd become even more of a hypocrite. He preached finding love, while he swore he'd never fall again.

The Prince of Hell sending a demon to murder the man of your dreams could have that effect on a guy.

Of course, Satan would say it was Gabe's own fault for falling in love with a human. And it was true sex demons rarely experienced love, but when Gabe met Jason, he couldn't help himself. Jason had no interest in sex. Zero. Zilch. Even when Gabe turned his magic on full blast, Jason wasn't fazed. Gabe was intrigued, to say the least.

Then what started out as mild interest quickly bloomed into friendship, which then turned into so much more.

When Satan caught wind of what was happening with his favorite incubus, he ordered Gabe to seduce and ruin Jason. When Gabe refused, Satan sent in another incubus, but Jason was immune to his powers too. Then the bastard sent a succubus. When he realized seduction didn't work, he resorted to more brutal tactics.

Jason had taught Gabe about emotions he never knew existed. That love was real, and it didn't require sex. Now that Gabe had his freedom, his mission was to spread the idea of emotional intimacy and stick it to Satan every chance he got.

And there he'd gone, falling down the rabbit hole of his past. He was so caught up in his thoughts, he didn't even realize he'd made it all the way to Frenchman Street until a brass band blasting out a jazz tune brought him back to the present. At ten in the evening, tourists milled about on the sidewalks, the street lamps casting their shadows long across the ground.

Pushing the unwelcome memories aside, Gabe ducked down the alley and entered The Tipsy Leprechaun. Cool air blasted his skin as he stepped through the door, and the scents of whiskey and beer greeted his senses. A band on a small stage in the corner played a pop hit while a group of witches danced and laughed in front of them. A gator shifter who looked like he'd had a few too many—his lopsided, shit-eating grin and hooded eyes gave him away—sat on a barstool ogling the women as they danced.

A petite redhead wearing a tight black dress winked at Gabe as he approached the bar, and warmth spread through his core.

"Hi. You're cute." She bit her bottom lip.

Even with his magic reined in, he was a good-looking guy, but this woman was downright sexy. His incubus mind presented him with a movie reel of all the luscious things he'd like to do to her...how many times he could make her scream his name before she couldn't remember her own.

Yeah, he still had the urges, but the price of his freedom meant he could never act on them. Satan had done him a favor on that one, though he'd never let the asshat downstairs know he'd actually helped him. He couldn't go around teaching intimacy without sex if he was getting it on every chance he got, could he? And he had chances galore...

He smiled and handed her a business card. "You're a beautiful woman who deserves to be loved unconditionally." And he was a total hypocrite.

Her brow furrowed, and as she looked down to read the card, he made his escape, striding to the opposite end of the bar. He checked the spot where he'd left his flyers, but the space sat empty. Good. Hopefully that meant his weekend retreat would be full. He already had twenty-eight supes signed up for the couples lecture tomorrow night. If things kept going this well, he might move to New Orleans permanently and make this his home base. Beelzebub knew there was nothing keeping him in San Francisco.

CHAPTER THREE

"The Cupid Ballroom? Can this guy get any more cliché?" Katrina rolled her eyes and marched through the hotel lobby before hanging a right toward her destination.

"Are you sure you want to do this?" Mike, a demon from her Hellions Anonymous group, hung back, not following her down the hallway.

She stopped and put her hands on her hips. "Yes, I'm sure. I refuse to let Satan or his irritating minion ruin everything I've worked for. I sank my life's savings into this app, and I am prepared to fight to the death for it."

He raked his fingers through his hair, glancing back toward the lobby. "You never said anything about fighting. Aren't you taking this too far?"

"You owe me one, remember? Or does it not matter that I'm the one who told your witch where to find you after you screwed up and damned her? You'd be making deals with the miscreants in L.A. if not for me."

Mike crossed his arms. "I suppose all the free meals I've given you at Honoré's weren't thanks enough?"

"C'mon, Mike." She dropped her arms by her sides, softening her tone. Mike was a friendly guy. He deserved better treatment than being the target of her wrath. "Please do this for me, and then we'll call it even. It's a couples session. All you have to do is check in with me. Then you can say you're going to whack off in the bathroom, or whatever it is guys do, and portal home."

His nostrils flared as he exhaled. "All right. But after this, we're even. No more free food. No more favors."

"Deal. Now come here and act like you like me." She linked her arm with his and led him toward the ballroom.

Katrina had fumed all day, waiting for this damn event to happen. Succubi weren't known for their patience, but now she could finally enact her revenge. Satan would *never* get the best of her.

A witch wearing the standard hotel uniform—a royal blue button-up and beige pants—met them at the door. "Names, please?"

"Tatiana Wiseman and Peter Finkle." Katrina winked at Mike, who rolled his eyes.

The witch nodded. "There are two seats left in the back row. Enjoy."

Katrina clutched Mike's hand and slunk inside, slipping into her seat without drawing attention, which was no easy feat for a succubus on the rampage. Mike sat next to her, glancing over his shoulder at the open door. She turned to see what he was looking at, and then he swiveled his head forward and laughed.

"Holy hellhounds. He's an incubus."

"What?" She jerked her head to the front of the room. While all fiends projected the same aura to the eyes of other supes, letting them conceal their magic, they couldn't hide it from other demons. Sure enough, the man taking the stage was a fucking incubus.

"Son of a bloodsucker," she whispered.

Mike shook his head, unbelieving. "Good luck with your revenge. I'm out." He waved his arm, creating a portal, and disappeared inside it.

Katrina sank in her seat, leaning to the left to hide behind a stocky werewolf. What in hell's name was Satan up to? Why on Earth would he send an incubus to teach celibacy classes?

She fought her growl as realization struck. The Devil was trying to teach *her* a lesson. To show her how ridiculous it was for a sex demon to swear off sex. And he just had to do it by sending the hottest man she'd ever laid eyes on. *Fucking Satan.*

Gabriel's magic wasn't showing in the slightest, but his deep blue eyes and strong jawline exuded sexy masculinity. His dark brown hair looked as soft as angel feathers, and her fingers twitched with the urge to touch it. Hell, she wanted to touch a lot more than his hair.

His voice was deep and smooth as honey, and she couldn't tear her gaze away from him as he spoke, which made her anger seethe into a cesspool of acid.

"Good evening. Welcome to the Emotional Intimacy for Couples lecture. My name is Gabriel Dakota, but you can call me Gabe."

Oh, she could think of plenty of things to call the sexy-as-sin nemesis—assubus, incubitch, her new immortal enemy. Satan's minion would be the one learning a lesson tonight. Never mess with a woman's livelihood.

She started small. As the incubitch—that was the best

name for him, since he was Satan's little bitch for doing this to her—gave his speech about feelings and friendship —*gag*—she let out a tiny bit of magic. It wasn't enough to be perceptible, even by the most skilled incubus, which he was *not*. But a man wrapped his arm around his girlfriend's shoulders while another rested a hand on his partner's knee. Before long, every couple there was holding hands or touching each other in some way.

Katrina couldn't fight her grin. She let out a little more magic, and a few people squirmed in their seats. A man in front of her adjusted his crotch. Gabe's brow furrowed, and he cleared his throat before inclining his head to peer into the audience. *Satan's balls*. He was already catching on. Incubitch was better than she thought.

Might as well go all-in now. Straightening in her seat, Katrina let her guise fully slip, and her magic pulsed through the room like an industrial-strength vibrator on high speed. A woman moaned. A man groaned. The couple closest to her started making out like a pair of teenagers beneath the bleachers at a high school football game.

"Stop!" Gabe's commanding voice drew the crowd's attention. "You're under a spell. You have to fight it."

A man in the front row spoke, "My wife hasn't looked at me like this in over a year. Give us more."

Gladly. Katrina sent out another pulse of magic, and the resulting collective gasp made her shiver. Even Incubitch wouldn't be able to resist that one. She leaned right to get a better view of her smokin' hot enemy, and sure enough, his lids fluttered on a deep inhale. His pants were too loose for her to see his bulge grow, but she knew—from experience—all incubi had dicks the size of wine bottles. Well, maybe not *that* big, but you get the idea.

It had been a while since she'd tasted an incubus…

Snap out of it, woman. He was here to ruin her; she wasn't about to offer him the best sex of his life as a reward. Though, with the way her body reacted to his, he might be the best she'd ever had as well. *Ugh!* She would need an ice bath to cool her jets after this. She was fasting for her freedom. No sex. Not even with her immortal enemy, no matter how hot hate sex could be.

Gabe visibly shuddered, and his guise slipped. *Aphrodite, have mercy.* If he was hot before, his true form was molten lava from the deepest pit in Tartarus. His cheekbones sharpened, his jawline somehow becoming even more masculinely defined, and his eyes… They flashed red briefly, and then the normal blue took on a sapphire sheen that could mesmerize Medusa. *Yum.*

He reined his magic in far too easily, turning hot-but-not-quite-as-hot, and set his jaw like a man on a mission. "Calm down, everyone. Do we have a demon in the room? An incubus or a succubus?"

Katrina scoffed. Like a demon would raise their hand and admit their magic to sixty supes.

"Oh, Andrew!" A woman threw herself into her partner's arms, and they tumbled to the floor, groping and dry humping each other like they couldn't get their clothes off fast enough.

Katrina snickered. *One more pulse of magic ought to do it.* Goosebumps rose on her skin as her power gathered in her core, and as she sent it out into the room, an erotic moan slipped from her lips. *Sweet Cerberus.* She might have overdone it this time.

Shirts started flying left and right. Moans and gasps filled the ballroom like a titillating symphony, and a pair of granny panties sailed through the air, landing right on

Gabe's face. *Perfect!* The incubitch's nostrils flared as he tossed the underwear aside.

Chairs toppled as people kicked them away to make more room on the floor. A woman straddled a man's lap, moving her arm in a circle like she was swinging a lasso, and he shouted, "Yee Haw!"

Okay, Katrina had done enough. Maybe a teensy bit too much, but that was what he got for trying to ruin her. It was time to make her exit. She rose to her feet as Gabe stomped down the aisle, and his gaze locked with hers.

"You!" He stopped two feet in front of her, his hands fisted at his sides. He was fuming so hard he might as well have had smoke rising from his skin.

Katrina grinned. "Well, hello there, handsome. This is quite a setup you've got here."

"Why the fuck are you doing this?" His eyes narrowed. "Did Satan send you?"

She crossed her arms. "Oh, please. We both know the devilish bastard sent *you* here to ruin me, so don't try to play games. There's only enough room for one sex demon in this town, and that demon is me."

He laughed cynically. "What is this, the Wild, Wild West? You want to meet me at high noon for a shoot-out?"

"I want you to leave this city and take your ridiculous 'emotional intimacy' lectures with you." She made air quotes. "This is your warning. Next time, I'll do a lot worse." She waved her hand, sliced open a portal, and went home to take that ice bath. Beelzebub knew she needed it.

Holy hellfire. Gabe sank into a chair and pressed a hand to his forehead as his clients fornicated on the floor. There was no stopping people once they'd been hit with a succubus's magic this strong. All he could do was wait it out until they were done.

This didn't make sense. Gabe had won his freedom. He'd paid the price, so Satan was supposed to leave him alone. It was part of the deal when a demon bargained for his release that he would keep his fiendish powers and urges—with only slightly more control—as a sort of punishment, but Satan would leave him to his own devices. The Devil never reneged on a deal, so something else was going on.

That something wasn't his most pressing concern at the moment, though. If word got out that his emotional intimacy classes turned out like this, his career would be over. Thankfully, he happened to know a powerful vampire who might be able to help.

Gaston had given Gabe his personal cell number when he checked in to the B and B, so he pulled out his phone and dialed it. The vampire answered on the second ring.

"Hey, man. I'm sorry to bother you." Gabe scooted to another chair to avoid being hit by a pair of naked shifters rolling over each other in the throes of their ecstasy.

"Is there a problem with your accommodations?"

If only it were something so small. "No, no. I'm at the hotel ballroom. We've had an incident, and I was hoping you could help me out with your vampire mind powers."

"An incident?" The music playing in the background on Gaston's end quieted. "I am intrigued and always down for a bit of debauchery. How many minds need wiping?"

Gabe blew out a hard breath. "About sixty. It's bad."

Gaston chuckled. "Say no more. I will bring rein-forcements."

"Thanks. I owe you one." Gabe returned the phone to his pocket and stood before moving toward the door. The last thing he needed was for one of the supernatural hotel staff—or worse, a human—to come inside and see the mess the succubus had made of his meeting.

That succubus… Satan sure knew how to pick them. She was easily the most beautiful woman he'd ever seen. She had thick, wavy brown hair that flowed like silk past her shoulders, and her lavender eyes pierced right through him, as if she could see into his soul and feel his desires.

Someone shouted, "Woo hoo *hoo*!" and Gabe rolled his eyes, leaning his head back against the door. At least it was consensual and they were all having fun. The succubus was right when she said she could do a lot worse. Still, this didn't bode well for their lesson on learning to appreciate each other on an emotional level.

Finally, after another fifteen minutes of copulation, his clients wore themselves out.

"I need everyone to get dressed now."

Of course no one listened. They all lay naked on the floor, their limbs in a tangle with their partners', their breaths coming out in pants. The low vibration of the succubus's magic still floated through the room. It would be a while before the supes returned to their senses. *Fucking fantastic.*

A knock sounded on the door behind him, and he cracked it open to find Gaston, Jane, and Ethan outside. He opened it a little farther so they could slip in, and then he pushed it shut behind them.

"Whoa." Jane surveyed the room and let out a low

whistle. "Talk about a bait and switch. After your description of the course, I was not expecting to see this."

"You should have led with the switch." Gaston rubbed his thumb and forefinger on his chin as he smirked. "I would have been the first in line to sign up for a lecture like this."

Gabe groaned. "This wasn't supposed to happen. I was ambushed by a succubus."

Amusement danced in his ice-blue eyes. "You don't say?"

"I know it's a lot to ask, but do you think the three of you could snap them out of this, get them dressed, and wipe the whole event from their minds?"

Jane toed a woman's leg with her shoe. When she didn't move, the vampire bent down to lift her arm and let it drop to the floor. "Damn. You weren't kidding when you said it was bad. I don't think even I could turn someone this unresponsive."

"You underestimate yourself, princess." Ethan rested a hand on her shoulder, and she rose to her feet.

"Never." She kissed him on the cheek. "We can do it. Right, Gaston?"

"Indeed. Shall I start at the front of the room, and you two can start from the back?"

"We'll meet you in the middle." Jane bent down again and held the woman's face between her hands. "Hey. Wake up and get dressed."

The woman's eyes blinked open, and she gasped. "What happened? Why am I naked?"

Jane stared into her eyes. "Nothing happened. The lecture was canceled, and refunds will be issued. Get dressed and leave."

Her gaze grew distant as she nodded. "Nothing happened. Refunds will be issued." She rose to her feet and put on her clothes while Ethan did the same routine on her partner. When they were both decent, they shuffled out of the room, looking confused as hell.

"Will they be okay?" Gabe asked.

"Oh, yeah," Ethan said. "It'll take a minute or two for the fog to lift, but they'll be fine."

"Are any of them vampires?" Jane rose and peered at the supes on the floor. "It's hard to tell with the succubus's magic still in the room… Which, by the way, Mr. Hottie McHottie Pants…" She looked at Ethan. "Vlad better get ready for a night of impaling when we're done here."

Ethan chuckled. "I can't wait."

Gabe cleared his throat. "No vampires in this session."

Jane gazed at her husband another moment before turning to Gabe. "That's good. Vampires can't glamour each other, so you might have had a problem."

"Is there anything I can do to help?"

"Make sure no one comes in," Ethan said. "What we're doing could upset the balance if anyone found out."

"Stupid truces." Jane rolled her eyes and moved on to a raven-haired witch. "They take all the fun out of being a creature of the night."

Gabe returned to his spot by the door and watched as his new friends cleaned up his mess. Well, technically, it wasn't *his* mess. That damn succubus needed to pay for what she'd done. Both literally and figuratively. He'd be out two grand once he issued all these refunds.

"This is the final pair." Gaston gestured to a couple of fae as they shuffled toward the door, and Gabe moved aside for them to exit.

"I can't thank you enough for your help with this," Gabe said.

Gaston nodded once. "This never happened."

"Please don't glamour me." Gabe closed his eyes. "I need to remember this so I can find that succubus and get even."

"Of course not," Gaston said, and Gabe opened his eyes. "How else will you recall the one you owe me if I make you forget?"

"Katrina really did a number on you," Jane said. "What did you do to piss her off?"

"You know her?"

Jane shrugged. "There's only one succubus in New Orleans that I'm aware of. She's a bit of a bitch too. I wouldn't want to be on her bad side."

"Do you know where I can find her?"

"She runs the Hellions Anonymous meetings at the Priscilla St. James Community Center on Thursday nights."

Interesting. "How long has she lived here?"

Jane looked at Ethan, who shook his head.

"More than one hundred years," Gaston said.

"So Satan didn't send her…" He checked the calendar on his phone. "The next meeting is tomorrow night."

Gaston grinned. "Oh, to be a bat on the wall at that meeting."

"I think you mean a fly on the wall," Gabe said.

Jane laughed. "No, he doesn't."

"How do you all know Katrina is a succubus? Do demons reveal their magic here?" Because if that were the case, he'd best move his operation elsewhere. No one would trust an incubus as a relationship counselor.

"No," Jane said, "but Katrina couldn't hide her nature if she tried. We figured it out the first time we met her."

That was a relief. "Well, thanks again for your help. I've got some refunds to issue, so I'm going to head back to the B and B." And once he took care of the damage Katrina had done, he'd figure out exactly how to make her pay.

CHAPTER FOUR

K atrina stood at the snack table in the Priscilla St. James Community Center meeting room, tapping her foot and drumming her fingers against her biceps. She focused every ounce of her energy into maintaining her soccer mom guise, but for all her effort, she still couldn't hide her magic.

"Hey, Katrina. Whoa." Richard stopped in front of her, his mouth falling slack. He used to be a famine demon back in the day, but now he had a potbelly so big it would take a crane to lift it and find his dick.

She let out a slow breath and tried to reel in her exposed magic. "Mike's not here yet. Go sit down."

"I'll do anything you want me to." Drool gathered on his lip.

Where the hell was Mike? He knew the demons of Hellions Anonymous relied on the mini angel food cakes he brought to the weekly meetings. The former Devil's advocate lived next door to Sweet Destiny's Bakery, and Destiny, an earth-bound angel, baked magic into the cakes that helped the demons subdue their fiendish natures.

Katrina's little stunt yesterday at the incubitch's lecture had done a number on her ability to stay in control. When her morning meeting with her app developer Antoine had ended with him shoving his hand down his pants, she'd hightailed it back home and stayed inside the rest of the day. Poor Antoine. He'd been mortified after she'd left and her magic had dissipated. He'd sent her six texts, apologizing profusely and begging her not to report him to HR.

Of course, she'd assured him she wasn't offended in the slightest—and she had no HR department to report him to—but when he wouldn't let it go, she had been forced to call him. *Ew.* Who used their phones to actually make calls these days? Once she'd confessed she was a recovering succubus and *she* should have been the one apologizing, he'd calmed down. Frankly, she was surprised he hadn't figured it out yet. It seemed every supe in New Orleans knew what kind of demon she was.

"Richard! Go sit down." She made a *shoo, go-away* motion with her hand, and he finally went on his way.

She continued her foot-tapping and focused on the drab beige wall in front of her. A registration table sat to the left of the door, and Sarah, a recovering pestilence demon, signed in before scribbling on a nametag and sticking it to her shirt. She wore a mask over her nose and mouth, but she took it off and shoved it in her pocket as she sank into a chair.

"Where's Mike?" Sarah pulled her blonde hair back into a twist and secured it with a band. "It's really hard to keep my magic in check these days." It must've been. Sarah had instigated the bubonic plague way back when by sneezing on a bartender in London. When the most recent pandemic started, everyone thought Sarah had fallen off the wagon, but she adamantly insisted she had nothing to do with it.

"He's late." Katrina's voice came out as a growl.

"I'm not late." Mike stopped at the sign-in table. "The meeting doesn't start for another five minutes." After sticking his nametag to his shirt, he sauntered toward the snack table at an excruciatingly slow pace and dropped a pastry box on the surface.

Katrina tore it open and snatched two cakes. She shoved one into her mouth before grabbing another, double fisting the angelic delicacies. An erotic moan escaped her throat as the magic took hold, and the tension in her muscles eased.

"Save some for the rest of us." Sarah approached the table and took a cake, biting into it and closing her eyes as she chewed. "Mmm… That's better. Thanks, Mike."

Katrina shoved the second cake into her mouth. Her cheeks puffed out like a chipmunk—they were supposed to be four-bite mini cakes, but whatever—and she smashed the pastry against the roof of her mouth with her tongue. It was light and fluffy, sweet but not too sweet, and she was finally able to reel in her succubus and complete her guise.

"Thank you, Mike. You have no idea how badly I needed that."

He cocked his head. "Did you…?"

"No. No, I'm still fasting, but it took a lot of magic to show that incubus who's boss around here."

He chuckled and shook his head. "I can't wait to hear about it."

Katrina nibbled on her third cake and took her seat in the "Circle of Hope," which was nothing more than a ring of metal folding chairs, but giving it the name was part of

HA rules. After setting her pastry on a plate in her lap, she addressed the room, "Good evening, everyone. Shall we begin?"

The other demons nodded.

"I'll start. Hi, my name is Katrina, and I'm a succubus."

"Hi, Katrina," they said in unison.

Everyone knew who she was. Hell, all the attendees had been in New Orleans for at least fifty years and knew more about each other than they cared to. But she always followed meeting protocol. They occasionally had a visitor from out of town, and she never knew when said visitor might be a board member doing an audit.

"I was banned from hell when Satan's flavor of the month found us in a compromising position in his chambers." She'd told the story so many times she said it word for word on autopilot. "Now, I run Swipe Right to Bite to help supes find others with...similar interests." As she finished, Mike cleared his throat and gestured with his head toward the door.

She turned around, and her jaw slammed shut with an audible click. There, sticking a nametag to his chest, was none other than Gabe the incubitch. He looked at her with a devilish grin, and she shot to her feet, fisting her hands at her sides. "You are not welcome here."

"Really?" He sauntered toward the circle with a cocky gait. "I thought all demons were welcome at, if not required to attend, HA meetings."

She crossed her arms, shifting her weight to her right foot. "You're welcome at your hometown meeting. You will *never* be welcome here."

He chuckled. "That's no way to treat a new member, is

it? New Orleans just may be my new hometown if you and I can set our differences aside."

"Our differences?" Her mouth fell open. "Are you insane? Satan sent you here to ruin me. How could I ever be okay with that? With you? You are Satan's bitch!" Okay, maybe that was a little harsh, but damn. Did he really think he could waltz into her town, do the Devil's bidding, and expect her to lean over the bathroom counter and take it from behind?

"I'm not his bitch. I gained my freedom decades ago. But…if you want to talk about a bitch…" He arched one of those thick, full brows drawing her attention to the deep blue of his eyes.

Focus, Katrina. She pressed a hand to her chest. "How dare you?"

"How dare *you*? What possessed you to come into my lecture and turn it into a sex-fest?"

A few of the demons in the group snickered, and Katrina jerked her head toward them, giving them a look that could freeze ice on the Devil's ass. That shut them right up.

"You're ruining my career! Thirty-five men have canceled their accounts on my dating app since you rolled into New Orleans. Do you know how much it's going to cost me? I rely on their monthly fees for my livelihood."

He laughed dryly. "Do you know how much it cost *me* to refund every ticket for the lecture you ruined?"

She lifted one shoulder dismissively. Maybe seductively. Hey, she was a succubus. Sex was never far from her mind. "Do I care?"

His brow slammed down over his sapphire eyes before they flashed red. Damn, he was sexy when he was mad.

Ugh! Why am I even thinking about him like that? He's my enemy.

"Obviously, you don't." He strolled into the circle and sat in an empty chair. "It seems we are at odds with the way we're atoning for our former sins. And if it's true there's only room for one sex demon in New Orleans, know this: I'm not going anywhere."

"Well, neither am I." Katrina plopped into her seat and crossed her legs. *The nerve!* Just who did this guy think he was strolling into her life, looking hotter than hellfire, and ruining everything she'd worked so hard to build?

He even had the gall to smile and give her a wink. "Hi. I'm Gabe, and I'm an incubus."

The other demons in the circle looked at Katrina for guidance. When she finally shrugged and rolled her eyes, gesturing to Gabe, they all said in unison, "Hi Gabe."

"Where should I begin?" He certainly wasn't ready to share his entire story with these people, especially with Katrina in the room. He had seethed all day, ready to…well, he wasn't sure what he was going to do…but hearing her story about how his business was affecting her, he could understand why she did it. He couldn't excuse her actions, but at least he knew the reason now.

When he didn't continue, a blonde demon raised her hand timidly. "We usually talk about why we wanted our freedom, and then we say what bargain we struck with the Devil."

Yeah, he definitely wasn't sharing all of that. "I fell in

love with a human, but Satan wanted me to ruin him. That's why I bargained for my freedom."

Katrina threw her head back and laughed like it was the most hilarious thing she'd ever heard. She had a beautiful laugh, musical, like bells. "Ha! That's a good one. Sex demons do not fall in love."

No wonder she had designed a hook-up app based on looks alone. She subscribed to the myth that succubi weren't capable of human emotion. He lifted his hands, palms up. "I did."

"Really…?" She tilted her head, amusement dancing in her lavender eyes. "And where is your human now?"

"He's dead, thanks to the Devil."

"I see. And what bargain did you strike to get your freedom?" She twirled a lock of silky hair around her finger.

He chuckled and crossed his arms. That was a bit of information he'd never revealed to anyone topside. "You can't expect me to tell all my truths in the first meeting. Who's next?"

"I'll go," an overweight famine demon said around a mouthful of food. He seemed oblivious to the tension between Gabe and Katrina, but the other demons kept their mouths shut, their gazes dancing between the two of them.

Gabe only half-listened to them as they shared their stories. Katrina completely ignored him despite his best efforts to catch her gaze. She was a stubborn, career-minded, drop-dead gorgeous woman, and he couldn't deny the spark of attraction burning in his chest.

Ridiculous, he knew, but it was there, nonetheless. He was angry with her, though, and he needed to remember that if he was going to get revenge. He had a mind to turn her meeting into an orgy, but that would be too easy. Besides, the demons here might appreciate it too much, and he wanted Katrina to squirm.

Oh, there was a thought…

"Something funny?" Katrina finally looked at him, and he realized he'd laughed out loud.

He shook his head. "Inside joke. I believe I interrupted you when I came in, Katrina, and I *always* let a woman finish."

Sarah's throat emitted a squeak at his words, but Katrina narrowed her eyes.

"What deal did you strike with the big guy downstairs to win your freedom?" he asked.

"I didn't." She gazed at her blood-red nails. "He won't set me free."

Nonsense. The Devil could never pass up a good bet. "Have you tried bargaining with him?"

"Of course I have. Many times." She inclined her chin defiantly.

"Satan is keeping her on reserve in case he can't get any in hell," Richard said.

"He wanted her to move in with him, but she shot him down," Sarah added.

Katrina shrugged. "He hasn't called on me in more than one hundred years. Eventually, he'll forget about me and my bond to hell will be broken."

Gabe suppressed a laugh. "That's not how the Devil works."

"That's what I've tried to tell her a dozen times," a demon with dark hair and brown eyes said. "And I should know. Hi, I'm Mike, and I'm a Devil's advocate."

"Hi, Mike."

As the rest of the demons told their stories, Gabe

formulated his plan. Wouldn't it be the ultimate stick-it-to-Satan act if he could get the Devil's former lover on board with emotional intimacy? And with her hook-up app out of the way, Gabe's business would boom.

Step one: He had to win Katrina over. She didn't have to like him, but she would have to *not* hate him if he was going to penetrate her defenses and convince her to join his side. What better way to do that than by helping her win her freedom?

There must have been *something* the Devil would value more than Katrina's servitude. If he could find out what it was, he could stick it to Satan from both ends by making the Devil an accessory to his plans.

CHAPTER FIVE

Gabe sat in the courtyard at the Bellevue Manor B and B, wringing his hands and working up the courage to pay the Devil a visit. He'd rather chew off his own dick than return to his former home—any recovering demon would—but if his life and career were going to work in New Orleans, he had to do this.

"Straight to the palace and back home." He nodded as if a simple head movement would make seeing Satan for the first time in decades okay. "In and out." As long as he didn't run into any of his old colleagues along the way, he'd be fine.

Before he could talk himself out of it, he rose and swiped a hand through the air, opening a portal. The sharp smell of sulfur assaulted his senses as the hot, sticky air from hell seeped through. He'd been topside so long, he'd forgotten how strong the stench was down below. A long, boiling hot shower would be in order when he got back to the surface.

He stepped through the portal, into the demons' entrance to hell, and it slammed shut behind him with a *whack.* Twinkling red and green lights lined the stone cavern, and the 1990s Halloween tape of tormented screams had been replaced by... Was that Christmas music?

"What fresh hell is this?" Gabe stilled, listening to the recording. He recognized the tune, but the words had been changed. A man with a deep voice crooned, "Satan's nuts roasting on an open fire," and Gabe laughed.

"You've got to be kidding me. It's the middle of summer." He shouldn't have been surprised. This was hell, after all.

As the song ended, the same voice picked up the tempo and sang, "Santa got run over by a vampire..."

Gabe shook his head and made his way down the stone path. It seemed the Devil was getting his kicks out of torturing demons now too. Go figure.

Keeping his head down to avoid any unwanted confrontations—and they were *all* unwanted down here— he strode past the new souls' general processing line. Hundreds of people stood in a queue, waiting to find out what level of the underworld their deeds in life had earned them. In the past, the wait was the torturous part, but now the people groaned and covered their ears as the music grew louder and the crooner sang, "We wish you a hellish afterlife" to a familiar tune.

Gabe picked up the pace, practically running by the time Satan's palace came into view. He much preferred canned screams over this nightmare they'd turned Christmas into. Tim Burton would be proud.

The obsidian castle hadn't changed from the outside. Turrets extended upward toward the rocky ceiling, and a moat of molten lava surrounded the Devil's lair. It bubbled and steamed, with the occasional spout of magma shooting out and sizzling on the ground. Good thing demons were impervious to heat.

"Hey," a voice called from behind him, and he turned to find a fellow incubus strolling down the path. "How's it hanging? Loose, I bet." The demon guffawed like he'd come up with the funniest joke known to hell.

It was nothing Gabe hadn't heard before. Word of his bargain had spread quickly in the underworld, thanks to Satan. He ignored the asshat and crossed the bridge extending over the moat to stand on the Devil's doorstep. Nausea churned in his stomach, much like the lava below. A bit of bile reached up to his throat, burning the back of his mouth, and he swallowed it down.

He pressed his palm to the hotplate on the exterior wall, and the lock *thunked* as it disengaged. When the ten-foot-tall door swung open, Gabe took in the red spires soaring six stories toward the ceiling. He'd half-expected to see a giant Christmas tree in the foyer, but apparently, that would have been too much, even for Satan. Blood-red drapes covered all the windows, blocking the view of hell from the inside, and Gabe made a sharp right, heading straight for the Devil's chambers.

His assistant, a stocky witch with long black braids, stopped him before he could knock on the door. "Do you have an appointment?" She held her thick brow low over her dark eyes like she had zero tolerance for bullshit.

"No, but I need to speak to Satan immediately."

"You can't see him without an appointment." She crossed her arms over her chest. "His next available slot is the Tuesday after Mardi Gras."

"That's more than six months away."

She shrugged and tossed her braids behind her shoulders. "The Devil is a busy man."

"Indeed." But Gabe couldn't wait that long. "What's your name? I've never seen you before. Are you new?"

"It's Rosemary, and I've been here a few months. Maybe a year. Time is relative down here."

"Well, Rosemary, it's nice to meet you. Satan has always chosen such beautiful assistants." He let his guise slip, hitting her with a pulse of incubus magic.

Her eyes glazed, and her lips parted on a gasp. "I…" She angled her head down and looked up at him, batting her lashes.

"I really need to see Satan now, love. Do you suppose I could *slip in and out*?"

She rubbed her neck, and he reined in his magic before she started rubbing something else. "Of course." Her voice was breathy. "Go right on in. I'll be here when you're done."

He stepped through the door, locking it behind him. It would be a hot minute before Rosemary recovered, but he didn't want to chance her storming in and dragging him out, which she looked stout—and mean—enough to do.

A fireplace stretched along the right wall, its flames licking upward to the ceiling, giving the room the illusion of being engulfed in an inferno. Gabe knew better. All Satan would have to do was clap his hands twice, and the fire would extinguish. The Devil loved his Clapper.

A high-backed leather chair stood behind a massive desk. It faced away from Gabe, and he could see Satan's ridiculous entrance coming from a mile away. He shook his head as the chair turned, and as expected, the Devil wore his signature red suit, his dark hair slicked back like a James Bond villain. He even held a fluffy white feline in his lap, and he stroked the animal's fur as he regarded Gabe. When did Satan get a cat?

"Gabriel, Gabriel." He continued stroking his pet, although on closer inspection, it had a demonic aura. What did that poor bastard do to deserve becoming Satan's house pet as punishment? "I'd say this is a surprise, but I heard about Katrina's efforts to sabotage your little class. She never disappoints."

"Good news travels fast," he mumbled.

"She is something else, isn't she?" He set the cat on the floor, and it darted beneath a sofa by the far wall. "Such an intriguing woman."

"She's something, all right."

"Please, have a seat." Satan leaned his elbows on the desk and steepled his fingers while Gabe sank into a leather chair. "What did you think of my new welcome soundtrack? Would you believe Santa Claus himself is the singer?"

"You don't say?"

The Devil nodded. "He recorded it after an incident in New Orleans last Christmas when he was accidentally turned into a vampire. I only wish I had been there to witness it."

"Sounds like a blast."

"Indeed." He leaned back in his chair and laced his fingers together. "But enough about me. I assume your return to hell isn't because you want your old job back?"

"You assume right."

He clicked his tongue. "Then your visit must have something to do with the delectable succubus you encountered in New Orleans."

"I—"

Satan held up a hand. "No, no. Don't tell me. Guessing is much more fun."

Gabe ground his teeth. Satan loved to play games, and while he would prefer to cut to the chase, he had to let the Devil have his fun before he could get the information he came for.

Satan's eyes lit up, and a wicked grin curved his lips. "Oh, Gabriel, this is just too rich. You're here to make a new deal, aren't you?"

"I need—"

"Now that you've met my favorite succubus, you've decided an eternity with a wet noodle in your pants is worse than you thought it would be."

His nostrils flared as he blew out a breath. "That's not—"

"You know I never go back on a deal, Gabriel. I gave you your freedom in exchange for you living the rest of your existence with erectile dysfunction. You agreed to the terms." He chuckled and shook his head. "I can see why you would ask, though. Katrina is a goddess between the sheets. The best I've ever had."

And Gabe could see why Satan didn't want to give her up if she was that good. Now if the gloating bastard would let him get a word in.

"But I'm looking for love, and sadly, she isn't the one for me. It's a shame, really." His gaze grew distant, and he finally shut his yapper.

"What would it take for her to gain her freedom?"

Satan inclined his chin, his brow lifting in surprise. "Don't tell me you're here to make a deal on her behalf. Have you fallen in love again?"

"No." His answer came too quickly, but he couldn't tell the Devil the real reason he wanted Katrina free. "I haven't known her long enough for love, but she's special to me." A special thorn in his side and pain in his ass.

"I'm afraid she has nothing to offer that's better than knowing I can have her anytime I want her."

"Nothing at all? What if she taught another succubus all her tricks? What if she could find you someone better?"

He laughed. "She's tried. She can't. There's no one quite like Katrina Alarie."

"Well, fuck." He dropped his hands on the arms of the chair.

"I'd ask if that were an offer, but your meat slinky wouldn't do it for me. When I'm in the mood for a bearded war hammer, I want it hard as steel." Satan slapped his hand on the desk and hooted with laughter.

Gabe rose to his feet, shame and anger battling for control in his chest. "I'm sorry for wasting your time." It was bad enough he couldn't get it up; he didn't need to withstand Satan's ridicule too. Yeah, he'd agreed to an eternity of impotence, but he wasn't any less of a man because of it.

"Wait. Wait." Satan gasped for breath. When he finally got himself under control, he continued. "I have an offer for you."

Gabe crossed his arms. "I'm listening."

The Devil rubbed his hands together. "Oh, this will be fun. You've heard of The Little Mermaid, have you not?"

"Yeah…"

"Ariel had three days to make Eric fall in love with her without using her voice. I will give you three weeks to make Katrina fall in love with you…without using your dick or telling her about this deal. Succeed, and she has her freedom. Fail, and one of your nuts goes into my collection." Satan shimmied his shoulders and laughed again. "It's not like they're doing you any good hanging between your legs!"

Gabe pursed his lips. Make Katrina fall in love... It would be wicked. Diabolical. Wrong on so many levels to toy with her emotions when he would never reciprocate the love. Then again, he was a demon. Wicked and diabolical was his nature.

If he could pull this off, he'd break her heart. But she'd have her freedom, which she would never achieve on her own. That would earn him her forgiveness. He could do this. He'd gotten a glimpse of her vulnerable side at the HA meeting, seen the spark in her eyes when she looked at him. It wasn't pure lust like the way others saw him. She was intrigued.

Satan danced in his chair, singing something about a one-eyed, one-horned, purple-headed yogurt slinger, and Gabe fisted his hands, straightening his spine in resolve.

"Double or nothing."

The Devil raised a brow. "Do go on."

"If I can make Katrina fall in love with me, she gets her freedom, and I get my dick back."

"Double reward means double the consequence if you fail. My offer is this: Make Katrina fall in love with you in three weeks' time. She *must* say the words aloud to you. If you succeed, she gets her freedom, and your flesh musket will fire again. Fail, and *both* your testicles become gold-laden paperweights for my desk."

Gabe swallowed hard. "Deal."

CHAPTER SIX

"It was frustrating, Jazz. You have no idea." Katrina lounged on Jasmine's couch and drummed her fingers on the pale blue fabric. A black and white photo of the St. Louis Cathedral hung on the wall across from her, and she curled her lip at the church. "It was like he got off on getting a rise out of me. You should have seen the look on his face."

Jasmine appeared from the kitchen, carrying two mugs of coffee. She offered one to Katrina and settled into a white accent chair. "I can imagine. He probably was getting off on it."

"The bastard." She sipped the coffee. It was dark and strong, just how she liked her men...if she were still having men, that was.

"Kinda like how you enjoyed sabotaging his lecture thingy. I mean, y'all *are* demons." She held her mug in both hands and inhaled the steam.

Katrina set her cup on the coffee table. "What are you trying to say?"

Jasmine held up a hand in defense. "Nothing. Nothing

bad but recovering demons do fall into the category of 'morally gray.' You can't fault him for the way he was made."

"I certainly…" She was about to insist she could fault him all she wanted for what he'd done, but her friend had a point. Demons weren't known for their morality. "I only sabotaged his operation because I thought Satan sent him. If I'd known it was a job he actually believed in, I…"

Jasmine smirked. "You'd have sabotaged him anyway."

Katrina pursed her lips. "Yeah, you're right. I can be a real bitch, can't I?"

"You *are* a demon." She shrugged and set her mug next to Katrina's. "I'm a necromancer who raises the dead, but my husband takes spirits to the underworld. Sometimes opposites attract. I bet if you talked to Gabe, y'all could work something out. Asher and I did."

"I don't know if I could stand his smug smile again. And his eyes…" They were *so* blue. Almost soulful. "Ugh! I can't tell if I want to rip his clothes off or punch him in the face."

"Maybe it's both."

She gave her head a tiny shake. It was neither. She needed to be rational about this. Her anger was getting the better of her, and she needed to chill the fuck out before all the work she'd done to subdue her demon went to shit.

She was only attracted to Gabe for two *very* inconsequential reasons. One: He was an incubus. Every woman —and man—in their right minds would find him mouthwateringly scrumptious. It was how he was made. Two: He was an incubus. She could sleep with him—not that she *would*, but she could—and her magic wouldn't ruin him in the slightest. Incubi were the only beings who weren't affected by her powers. Okay, so it was one reason.

Of course, if Satan would set her free, she'd be able to control her magic and not ruin every person she banged, but the bastard refused. He was the Prince of Hell, for fuck's sake! He could get any woman he wanted, but nooo… Fasting was the only option she had now. Although Gabe could serve as a cheat day…

Nope. She was not going there. Not with him. *Satan's balls.* She was only attracted to him because he was an incubus, just like the spark in his gaze when he looked at her was there because she was a succubus.

Jasmine picked up her mug and took another sip. "Either way, I still think—"

Katrina's phone buzzed on the table, her tech support guru's name lighting up the screen. "Hold that thought."

She hit the speaker button. "Hey, Celeste. How's it going?" See? She could be nice when she wanted to.

"We've got an issue with a new subscriber that needs escalation." The sound of keys clacking emanated from the background on Celeste's end.

"I'm not very good at the tech side of this. What's the problem?"

She laughed. "It's not tech. This guy just joined two days ago, and he's upset because he hasn't gotten any matches yet. I assured him there's nothing wrong with the programming, but he insists on talking to you."

Katrina's lips fluttered as she blew out a breath. "He's probably butt ugly and doesn't know how to use the filters to make himself look better. Forward the chat thread to me, and I'll take care of it."

Celeste hesitated before she replied, "Okay, but be gentle with him."

She looked at Jasmine, who suppressed a smile. "I'm always gentle."

Jasmine busted out with a laugh that could have woken the dead. Then again, that was her job so…

Katrina gave her the stink eye before speaking into the phone. "I promise to go easy on him."

"I'll send it over in a few."

"Thanks, Celeste." Katrina ended the call and picked up the paperback novel lying on the end table. The cover consisted of the title centered over a man's bare chest. She flipped it over and read the description on the back. "A romance novel, Jazz? Don't you get enough of this stuff with your man?"

"Of course I do, but the books are still fun to read."

Katrina pulled a face. "What's so fun about two people falling in love? It sounds incredibly boring to me."

"There's plenty to love about romance. They always end with a happily ever after, so you know you're not going to feel gutted at the end. They're good for stress relief because you can check out of the real world for a while. The ones I read also have plenty of sex…" She sang the last part as if that should be reason enough for a succubus to enjoy the books.

Katrina opened the novel and flipped through the pages. Okay, the sex part did pique her interest.

"Maybe you should take that one home and give it a try. You might like it."

She blew a hard breath through her nose. "Doubtful. There is no such thing as happily ever after for a succubus."

"Then live vicariously through the characters. Who knows? Maybe reading about people falling in love and all those pesky emotions that go with it will help you be less of a bitch."

"I suppose I could use a little help in that department." She tucked the book into her purse. "I'll give it a whirl."

Her phone pinged, and she picked it up to find the unhappy customer's information. "Let's see what dog face man's problem is."

Jasmine moved to sit next to her on the couch and peered at the screen. "Surely he can't be *that* bad. Maybe he's a shifter who used a picture of his animal instead of his human face."

Katrina navigated to his account and laughed. "There's his problem. He used a sunset. Nobody wants to hook up with a flaming ball of gas."

"Look at his profile," Jasmine said. "He chose 'prefer not to answer' for every physical descriptor, including what kind of supe he is."

"Hmm…" Katrina narrowed her eyes at the screen. Something about this felt off. "Why do I find Mr. Rene Boudreaux highly suspicious?"

"What do you mean?"

She scrolled through the other men's profiles. "Look at these. They all have photos that are either up close face shots or waist up showing their physique. One can gather by which they chose whether or not they have body image issues."

Jasmine lifted one shoulder. "Or maybe they don't want to be judged on their physique alone."

"You're forgetting the purpose of this app. All they get to attract a date is a picture and a few physical descriptors. I purposely didn't include an input field long enough for them to write a paragraph about themselves, so the picture is *everything*."

"Why didn't you?"

"Because bios are lame, and people always lie in them.

How many times can you read 'I'm a kind-hearted man who likes puppies and long walks on the beach' before you vomit?"

"I see your point. So, what do you think is up with this guy?"

Katrina shot his profile a narrow look as her kindling of suspicion ignited into a flame. "I think Mr. Boudreaux isn't Mr. Boudreaux."

She blinked twice. "You think this is Gabe, don't you?"

"I know it is. I sabotaged his lecture, so he's going through my app to get revenge. It's exactly what I would do if our roles were reversed." *Touché, Mr. Dakota. Or should I call you Mr. Boudreaux?*

"What do you think his plans are?"

"We're about to find out." She opened the messaging app and typed her inquiry.

"Hello, Mr. Boudreaux. My name is Katrina Alarie. Tech support has escalated your issue to me. I understand you're unhappy with your results on the app. Please, tell me how I can be of assistance."

His reply came a moment later, *"I've been on the app for two days, and I haven't received a single match. I believe your software may have a bug."*

She responded, *"We've run a thorough diagnostic. I assure you, Mr. Boudreaux, that our software is running in tip-top shape."*

"Did you really run a diagnostic?" Jasmine asked.

Katrina shrugged. "How should I know? I'm the creative genius in this operation. I pay people to handle the technical stuff."

"What if this isn't Gabe? What if it's a regular guy? The poor sap might be clueless…"

She shook her head. "It's Gabe. Just wait for it."

He replied, *"Then how do you explain my lack of connections? I heard you have eighty percent of the single supes in New Orleans on this app."*

"See? That's technical information only someone looking to destroy me would take the time to research."

"I don't know…" Jasmine sounded skeptical, but Katrina was absolutely positive. Call it demon intuition if you want, but she *knew* this was Gabe.

She sent another message. *"I've had a look at your profile, and I believe the issue lies there. Your photo is a sunset, and you offered no physical descriptors. It would be irrational to expect someone to swipe right on your profile when they don't even know what you look like or what kind of supe you are."*

She smiled smugly as she hit send. "Here it comes. The definitive proof."

Three little dots bounced on her screen as she waited for his reply. It was taking forever. No doubt he was formulating some ridiculous story about looks not being important. What was his endgame, though? Did he think he could get her to change the setup of her app? If so, he was sorely mistaken. Eighty percent of the single supes in New Orleans couldn't be wrong.

His reply finally came through. *"I didn't include the physical descriptors because I prefer to get to know a potential date before the relationship becomes physical."*

"Bingo!" Katrina showed Jasmine the screen. "Can I say, 'I told you so' now?"

Gabe sent another message. *"As for what kind of supe I am, I also prefer for a potential date to get to know me as a man first. After all, dating apps are human technology."*

Katrina threw her head back and laughed. What point was he trying to prove? "Oh, Gabe. I thought you were smarter than this. I'm probably not the first person to overestimate you."

"Holy ghost guts." Jasmine chuckled, unbelieving. "He can't get more obvious than that, can he? Are you going to call him out?"

"Oh, no. That would be letting him off way too easily. I'm going to toy with him for a while."

Jasmine shook her head. "Of course you are."

"I'm a demon. What did you expect?" She typed a reply, *"At the moment, this app is designed for physical attraction to be the initial factor. If an emotional bond forms afterward, that's entirely up to the matched pair when they meet. I might consider adding a bio section where users can include a bit about their personalities, but I'm not convinced that's the direction I want to go."*

Yes, she'd just told her friend why she purposely left that field off, but Gabe didn't need to know that.

His response was as she expected, *"I think it would be a beneficial addition. Looks alone should never be a deciding factor in a relationship. Is there anything I can do to convince you?"* He had taken the bait.

"Well, Mr. Boudreaux. Why don't you tell me what you might want people to know about you if they were given the opportunity to get to know you as a person before anything else."

"What's your plan?" Jasmine asked.

Katrina brushed her hair behind her shoulders. "It's simple. I'm going to make him fall for me. Then, when he's wrapped around my finger, he'll cancel his stupid therapy sessions and be out of my hair for good."

"Is it possible for an incubus to fall for someone?"

"He seems to think so."

CHAPTER SEVEN

"Game on." Gabe grinned as he read Katrina's last text. She was a businesswoman above all else. Well, she was trying to be anyway. His plan to penetrate her defenses by masquerading as a disappointed customer was the perfect way to get to her...*You've Got Mail* style. Now the trick was to tell her just enough about himself for her to be intrigued without giving away his identity. He'd purposely waited a few days to enact his plan, lying low and avoiding any encounters with her so she wouldn't be suspicious.

He pursed his lips and stared at his phone screen. He should have come up with a bio before he initiated his scheme. It needed to be good, to make him appear dashing and mysterious without being cliché. Katrina seemed like a woman whose bullshit tolerance would be negative twenty at best.

The band on the patio at Café Du Monde struck up a jazzy tune just as the server delivered Gabe's café au lait with a plate of beignets. The famous bakery, situated between the Mississippi River and Decatur Street, was high on his list of places to visit. A line of tourists stretched down the sidewalk at all hours of the day, and he could imagine how long they had to wait to get a table beneath the iconic green and white awning. He only had to imagine because when he asked the host in charge of seating if he had a table available, all it had taken was a flirtatious wink for the man to seat him immediately.

Hey, what was the use of being a magical being if he never got to use his magic?

He set his phone down and sipped the half-milk, half-coffee-with-chicory concoction so many people raved about. *Mmm...* The milk tamed the bitterness of the coffee perfectly. He could see the appeal.

Now, what to tell Katrina? He thought back to Jason and how a human had made an incubus fall in love. Aside from his disinterest in sex, which had been the initial intrigue that made Gabe want to know more, Jason had *listened.* He'd asked Gabe questions about himself and remembered his answers. Jason had been interested in Gabe as a person. Perhaps that was where he should start with Katrina.

He chuckled and grabbed his phone to type a message, *"Ladies first. What would you want people to know about you before anything else?"*

While he waited for her reply, he picked up a beignet and took a bite. The rectangular French pastry was deep-fried and covered in a mountain of powdered sugar, which rained onto the table and all over his pants. *Lovely.* They were messy but so worth it. He took another bite, and Katrina's reply came through.

"You forget... You're supposed to be convincing me why I should include a bio section in my app. If you can't even think of what you would say, I rest my case. They're not necessary."

"I see how you're going to be…a tough nut to crack." He cringed. Both of his nuts were on the line, and unless he wanted to see them roasting over an open fire and dipped in gold, he had to make this happen.

"I would say I'm a good listener."

Her reply came instantly, *"Who wouldn't?"*

"I'd say I enjoy staying in as much as I like going out."

"Boring."

He ground his teeth. What did she want from him? Three dots bounced on the screen, and he picked up his half-eaten beignet, shoving the entire thing into his mouth.

"If you'd like to cancel your account, I will issue a refund for your first payment."

"Oh, no. That's not happening." He typed a reply, *"I don't want to cancel. It's been decades since I've found myself interested in another person, and I was hoping this app would help me get back out there."*

He hit send and bit his lip. *Good going, dumbass.* He was supposed to make himself sound mysterious and intriguing, not desperate. And it was a lie to boot. Well, only a half-lie. It was true he hadn't been interested in anyone in decades—aside from his incubus urges to fuck everything in sight—but he definitely wasn't looking to get back out there. One broken heart was enough, thank you very much.

Katrina replied, *"You have my attention."*

Interesting… So she liked vulnerability in a man. Duh, of course she did; she was a succubus for Beelzebub's sake. It was her nature to prey on the weak and vulnerable, much like it used to be his.

How to handle this? Show her his sensitive side right out of the gate or backpedal and put on a macho façade?

Vulnerable was what caught her interest. Hopefully, it would set the hook too.

"I'm looking for someone who will stay up late with me talking, telling me everything about themselves." He held his breath as the three little dots bounced again.

"And now you've lost it. This is why I don't include bios. No one is authentic, and they resort to the most cliché things imaginable."

Fuck me. He needed to redeem himself quickly. He started to type in a reply, but another message from Katrina came through, *"Tell you what, Mr. Boudreaux. I'll give you one more chance. Write a bio…an authentic bio… and send it to me. If I'm intrigued, we'll talk again. You have twenty-four hours."*

"I'm not sure you understand the concept of getting to know someone on an emotional level." Jasmine took their empty mugs to the kitchen and set them in the sink.

Katrina waved her hand flippantly. "He's an incubus. He may think he's looking to fall in love—and it's probably possible for him since he's free from Satan's rule—but at his core, he's a sex demon. We prey on the weak, so he needs to see that I'm strong or he won't respect me."

Jasmine tilted her head. "That's insightful for a demon, Katrina. I'm impressed."

"I can be deep when I want to be…and not just with my throat." She smirked, and Jasmine laughed.

"Gabe just admitted he's looking for love, so that's what I'm going to make him think he's getting. I have the hook, but I need your help being the bait."

Jasmine returned to the living room and sank into a chair, folding one leg beneath her. "How so?"

"Once he sends me his bio, which will be full of vulnerabilities, I'll need your help in exploiting them."

"I'm not really the exploiting people type."

"Let me rephrase then. I will need your assistance in deciphering his love language so that I may give him what he needs." *Ick.* Did those words just come out of her mouth? She rolled them around in her mind a few times to see if the bitter flavor would subside. Nope. She was still a succubus through and through.

"If you want him to fall in love with Katrina, you need to *be* Katrina."

"Yes, but Katrina doesn't know how to give. That's where you come in. You can help me figure out what he would want to hear."

"He needs to hear from *you*, not me. Just be yourself."

"Be myself?" She crossed her arms and drummed her fingers against her biceps. "That's the best advice you can give your BFF? Seriously?"

Jasmine sighed. "Be kind. Be honest. Show him that you care about his needs."

Katrina opened her mouth with a retort, but she couldn't think of one. Kindness and honesty were two traits a succubus never needed. She clasped her hands in her lap and looked into her friend's eyes. "I don't know how. Will you help me?"

Sympathy crinkled her brow. "Suffering spirits, I've got my work cut out for me."

"Well, if you don't want to…"

She held up her hands. "I'm kidding. Katrina, you do know how. You're kind and honest with me, aren't you?"

She lifted one shoulder. "That's different. You're my

friend."

"So, treat Gabe like a friend."

"But he's supposed to fall in love with me."

"And he will, but you have to make him like you before he can love you."

"I see your point." This was going to be harder than she thought. Jasmine was probably the only person in New Orleans who truly liked her. She'd never bothered trying to win anyone else's affections.

"Go home and read the novel. If you want to experience two people falling in love and living happily ever after, without going through it yourself, that's the best place to start."

Katrina rose and went to Jasmine's bookshelf. "You're right. I need to do my research, and one book won't be enough. May I borrow a few more?"

"Take all you need."

She gazed at the books. There must have been fifty on the shelf. "Where do I begin?"

"Let me help." Jasmine began taking novels from the bookcase and handing them to her. "This one is friends-to-lovers. Those are always sweet. Here's an alpha billionaire, and this one is a best friend's brother. Oh, this one is a fake relationship. That sort of applies, right?"

"I suppose."

"It's not the one I'm looking for, though. Here's a workplace romance with the boss/employee power dynamic going on." By the time Jasmine found the book she was looking for, Katrina's arms were full of paperbacks.

"Aha! This is my all-time favorite enemies-to-lovers novel." She started to put the book on the top of Katrina's stack but clutched it in both hands instead. "Actually, no. You probably shouldn't read this one. Not yet."

"Why not? It sounds like the perfect lesson for me. How to turn my enemy into my lover."

"Yeah, but enemies-to-lovers isn't the best research material for actual enemies. This couple gets together in spite of themselves. They fight it every step of the way. You need to try some with a little less angst to start."

"Oh, pish. I'm a big girl; I can handle it." She nodded toward the books. "Put it on the stack."

"I don't know."

Katrina rolled her eyes and let out a dramatic sigh. "I promise not to read it first, okay?"

Jasmine gave her a skeptical look, screwing her mouth over to the side.

"Cross my heart." She batted her lashes for emphasis, and her friend dropped the novel onto the stack.

"Do you want a bag for those, Miss Pants on Fire?"

"Nah. Just hand me my purse." She balanced the books in one hand, resting her chin on top of the pile to keep them from toppling over. After Jasmine looped Katrina's purse strap over her shoulder, she sliced her hand through the air, opening a portal. "Thanks for the advice, Jazz. I knew I could count on you."

"I'll want those back!" Jasmine called as Katrina stepped through the portal and into her own living room.

The moment it slammed shut behind her, she marched to the kitchen and dropped the books on the table. She put a bag of popcorn into the microwave and grabbed last night's half-empty bottle of chardonnay from the fridge. Gabe had twenty-three hours left to send her his bio, and she was determined to make it through at least one of Jasmine's mind-numbing romance novels before he did. She grabbed the enemies-to-lovers one off the top and flipped it over to read the description.

When the microwave dinged, she took her snack, wine, and the forbidden book to the couch and propped her feet on the coffee table. Hey, Jasmine knew when she relented and gave Katrina the book it would be the first one she read. She was a demon, for Beelzebub's sake. She couldn't help her nature.

Before she could crack open the novel, her doorbell rang. With a sigh, she got up and padded through the foyer. A quick peek through the peephole revealed the other occupant in her duplex, old Ms. Humphreys. It wasn't fair to call her old. Katrina had been around centuries before her human neighbor was even a glimmer in her daddy's eye, but Ms. Humphreys' curly hair was so gray it was almost white, and her dark brown, wrinkled skin looked thin and frail. Still though, her dark eyes sparkled when she smiled, and her laugh lines ran deep.

Katrina opened the door. "Good evening. What can I do for you?"

Ms. Humphreys grinned and looked over her shoulder as if making sure no one was passing by on the sidewalk. "Do you have any batteries I could borrow?"

"Sure. Come on in. What size do you need?"

Ms. Humphreys pulled the door shut and waited in the foyer as Katrina went to the kitchen junk drawer. "C. Two if you have them."

She gave her a knowing look. "C, you said? Are they for a radio?"

Her neighbor giggled. "I had a hot date, but he forgot to take his Viagra, so I sent him home."

"Ms. Humphreys..." Katrina chuckled and grabbed the batteries. "Men do lose their usefulness when their dicks stop working, don't they?"

"If the trouser trout is floppy, it's time to throw it back

to the sea."

Katrina handed her the batteries and winked before locking the door behind her and returning to her position on the sofa.

The book started out much as she expected, introducing the characters and setting up why they were enemies and why nothing could ever work between them, but it was so obvious they wanted each other. The sexual tension was off the charts hot, and Katrina found herself first rolling her eyes and wondering why the hell they didn't just do it already and then yelling at the characters that if she had balls, they'd be blue by now. She might have to follow Ms. Humphreys' lead and break out her own toys when this was done.

"These people are idiots!" Halfway through, they *finally* got together, and yes, Katrina did enjoy the sexy scene very much, thank you. But then there was regret and angst and miscommunication, and her metaphorical balls turned blue again.

She needed a refill and more food, but she couldn't leave the couple hanging like this. She *had* to know how it would end. She read, turning page after page and absorbing all the vivid details. When she got to the end, and the couple did, in fact, get to live happily ever after, she might or might not have shouted, "Yes!"

Her ears burned, and she closed the book, looking around as if someone might have snuck into her home and witnessed her little display of emotion. She returned to the kitchen for her refill and put a frozen pizza into the oven.

Honestly, there was no reason for her to be embarrassed that she'd enjoyed a book more than she thought she would. She ran a dating app. Maybe she wasn't helping people find true love, but knowing more supes were out there having fun and getting laid did warm her heart. Yes, demons had hearts.

Of course, the four very detailed sex scenes helped, but the story itself was good too. It gave her hope that someday, after she'd won her freedom, she might be able to experience a bit of romance herself. Maybe even love.

She sat on the kitchen counter, reading the next book on the pile as she waited for her pizza to finish cooking. When the timer dinged, she took the rest of her wine and the book back to the couch and settled in for another story. The second book was even more intriguing than the first. She should have been taking notes about all the ways the couples showed their emotions and what attracted them to each other, but she couldn't be bothered.

When she finished book number two, she moved on to a third, and she kept reading until she couldn't hold her eyes open another minute.

A buzzing sounded from the coffee table, and Katrina snorted. She opened her eyes to find she'd fallen asleep on the couch, lying on her side and using the open book as a pillow. Drool trailed from the corner of her mouth onto the pages, and as she sat up, they stuck to her skin.

"Oh, fabulous." She peeled the book off her face and stood to look in the mirror. Her hair was a tangled mess, her drool had left a crusty white stain, and the words from the page were tattooed in reverse across her cheek. "How long was I out?"

She glanced at the clock. Fabulous. She'd stayed up all night and slept most of the day. Who knew romance novels could be so addictive?

She swiped her phone open on the table as she sank onto the sofa, and her pulse sprinted. Gabe had sent his bio.

CHAPTER EIGHT

Gabe pressed send, set his phone on the nightstand, and walked across the room to sit by the window overlooking the courtyard. He'd toiled over that stupid bio for hours, convinced it was his only shot at making Katrina fall for him. If he couldn't worm his way into her heart anonymously, he'd be screwed…and not in the fun way.

Why he had such a hard time coming up with something to write, he wasn't sure. He taught people how to open themselves to emotional intimacy, for fuck's sake. But it was different when he was personally involved. Gabe *wasn't* open to emotional intimacy. Not anymore.

And dating app bios… Katrina was right. There was no way to sum himself up in three to four sentences without sounding like a cliché douchebag.

He stared out the window, waiting for Katrina's reply. Gaston's backyard was immaculate, with trimmed grass and perfectly shaped hedges surrounding a stone fountain in the center. A pair of cougar shifters on vacation from Texas sat on a bench beneath a magnolia tree, and the man plucked a large white bloom from a branch, bringing it to his nose before offering it to his mate. She accepted the token, smiling and resting her head on his shoulder as he wrapped his arm around her.

That was the kind of relationship Gabe advocated. The kind he helped people achieve so he could atone for his centuries as an incubus. The kind Satan despised.

Ten minutes went by with no reply from Katrina, so he grabbed his phone to reread the message he'd sent.

"I'm not like other men. Or maybe I am. Depends on the men you know. I assume, since you're on a dating app, you haven't had the best of luck with relationships. Neither have I. Let's face it—dating is hell. Believe me, I've been there and back again, but the road to happily ever after isn't smoothly paved. I'm willing to hit a few potholes to get there. Are you?"

He rolled his eyes and groaned. Talk about cliché metaphors. Katrina probably hadn't replied—wouldn't reply—because she was too busy laughing her ass off. He was about to begin formulating a different plan when the three little dots of anticipation danced on his screen. Clutching his phone, he sank onto the edge of the bed as her reply came through.

"I like your frankness, Mr. Boudreaux, but I'm still not convinced a bio would benefit the users of my app. Not everyone is looking for love."

He'd heard that line so many times, his answer came instantly, *"You don't have to go looking for love. If you're open to it, it will find you eventually."*

"What if I don't want to be found?"

Good. She phrased her question in the first person. Now he was getting somewhere. *"Why wouldn't you want happiness? Love is such a fulfilling emotion."* And I am such a hypocrite. He didn't want to be "found" either, yet here he was, pushing the concept on her like he did to all his clients. Although, his clients came to him because they wanted to. They were looking for change. Katrina wasn't.

Did he feel bad about what he was doing? A little bit, yeah. But he'd sealed the deal with Satan because his masculinity had been mocked. He'd let his emotions get the better of him, and now Katrina's freedom—and the rest of his manhood—were on the line.

Five minutes went by with no reply. The dots didn't even bounce. What was she thinking? He was tempted to send another message, but his question wasn't an easy one for a sex demon to answer. He needed a distraction, so he wandered down to the living room and found Gaston filling a carafe with blood.

The vampire gestured to the container. "Breakfast?"

Gabe chuckled. "The eggs you made this morning were plenty. Thanks."

When did this guy sleep? He was up at daylight making food for his non-nocturnal guests, and he was up again hours before nightfall to prepare the meal for the vamps.

Gabe's phone buzzed with a message from Katrina: *"One can find happiness without love. You're assuming a person is incomplete without a partner, and that couldn't be further from the truth. Plenty of people have rich, fulfilling lives without romance. Happiness comes in many forms."*

Well, damn. She had a point. An eloquently stated point. From a succubus still under Satan's command, he'd expect an answer along the lines of "Sex good. Love bad." Perhaps there was more to Katrina than met the eye.

"Are you okay?" Gaston asked.

"Yeah, it's...work stuff." He sank onto the sofa to contemplate his rebuttal.

Gaston arched a brow as he sat across from him. "Are you certain? Your face is pinched like…" He grinned. "As Jane would say, like you are constipated."

Gabe laughed. "I'm fine. I'm trying to coach a stubborn client."

Gaston leaned back, propping his ankle on his knee. "Male or female?"

"Female."

He nodded knowingly. "I love a stubborn woman. Their strength gives them an appeal that turns my engine on."

Gabe started to ask if Gaston meant they got his motor running, but he refrained. The vampire's quirks were his own. Who was he to correct him?

"This one is stubborn *and* smart as hell. I've got my work cut out for me."

"Nothing worthwhile is easy to obtain."

"Very true." Now how to word his reply to Katrina?

"You are absolutely right. Happiness does come in many forms, and your app helps people achieve one aspect of it."

"I'm glad you agree."

"But…" He grinned. How would she answer this one? *"Hook-ups are only temporary happiness. What are you doing to help the people who want more?"*

"It's no secret I'm a demon. Helping people isn't my concern."

He knew that wasn't true. If she didn't care about helping people, she wouldn't be running the weekly HA meetings. She also wouldn't have started her dating app, to begin with. Even if she did think casual sex was the best sex, she was still helping people find it. Katrina was deep, much more complex than the wicked woman who'd sabotaged his lecture, and he couldn't wait to peel away the layers.

He typed his reply, *"I don't think you mean that. I think you enjoy helping people."*

"You don't know me."

"I think I do. I'd like to know you more."

"You think you do? How, if we've never met?"

"Maybe we should meet."

A good five minutes passed before she responded: *"I will consider it, but now I have work to do. Have a good evening, Mr. Boudreaux."*

"Please, call me Rene."

"Fuck me bending over backwards." Katrina tossed her phone on the table and wiped her hands on her jeans. She had enjoyed that argument a little too much. Well, it wasn't really an argument. It was more like a debate, but whatever. It turned her on, nonetheless. It had been a while since she'd had an intelligent back and forth with a man.

Strange that he suggested meeting in person so soon, though. Even stranger that she said she'd consider it. Perhaps he was simply testing her. Or maybe she'd already piqued his interest enough that he wanted to see her. Either way, it didn't matter. They needed more texting time for her to warm him up.

She cleaned up her dinner mess and headed to the shower so she could salvage what was left of the day. With her hair in a messy bun and her comfy clothes on, she settled behind her laptop to check on her business.

All the fun she'd experienced in her banter with Gabe

quickly turned sour when she found fifteen women had canceled their accounts on her app today. "I've got to work faster on that man."

She shot Antoine an email, asking him to meet with her tomorrow to work on retention. Maybe adding a bio section to the profiles wouldn't be such a bad idea while Gabe was in town. At least then her users would feel like they were looking for more than a hook-up. If it didn't help, she could have it removed.

In the meantime, she would enact operation flirtation with Mr. Boudreaux/Dakota, and to accomplish that, she needed to do more research. She grabbed two more novels from Jasmine's stack and settled onto the sofa for another evening of reading.

Halfway into the second book, she smelled smoke. Ms. Humphreys must've burned her dinner again. It wouldn't be the first time Katrina's side of the building had suffered the consequences of her neighbor leaving the roux on the stove too long. She read another page or two when a crackling sound emanated through the dividing wall.

"What is that woman doing?" She set the book down and stood, and that was when she finally realized she didn't just smell smoke; her apartment was full of it. Hey, she was born and raised around fire and brimstone. Cut her some slack.

Smoke gushed through the air vent, and flames followed, licking across the ceiling. "Oh, for fuck's sake. I got enough of this in hell." She dialed 9-1-1. "Hello, my home is on fire."

"Were you able to get out?" the operator asked.

"Oh. Well, I haven't yet, but I will. I'm not so sure about my neighbor, though."

"I've dispatched the fire department. Can you get out and check on your neighbor?"

"Of course. Yes." Ms. Humphreys was probably standing on the front porch ranting about her gumbo being ruined again. She stepped out of her apartment and found an excited crowd gathering on the street.

"Is there anyone else inside?" a man shouted at her. Ms. Humphreys was nowhere in sight.

Katrina stepped onto the sidewalk to see what the commotion was about. Black smoke poured from the windows, and flames had already crumbled part of the roof. A siren wailed in the distance.

"Ma'am? Did your neighbor make it out?" the operator asked.

"She's not in the front. I'll check the back door." Katrina darted up the front steps.

"Don't go back inside!" a woman yelled. Seriously, what was it with all these people yelling at her? The fastest way to the backyard was through the house.

"Ma'am, don't go back inside," the dispatcher said, and Katrina hung up the phone. She'd had enough of people telling her what to do.

Smoke engulfed her entire living room, and if she wasn't a demon, she would have choked and possibly sweated to death on her way to the door. When she reached the back porch, she found Ms. Humphreys' door closed. She must've been trapped inside. *Whoops.* Katrina glanced around to be sure no one could see her before portaling into her neighbor's home.

Poor Ms. Humphreys sat cowering on the floor beneath her dining table. Sweat poured down her face, and she had pulled her shirt up to cover her nose.

Katrina kneeled in front of her and opened her arms. "Come on, dear. Let's get you to safety."

Ms. Humphreys crawled out from beneath the table, and Katrina wrapped one arm around her before opening a portal with her other. Her neighbor gasped—which wasn't a good idea in a room full of smoke—and Katrina pulled her through the opening and into the backyard.

She held her, rubbing her back as the old woman hacked up the smoke. "There, there. You'll be okay."

When she finished coughing, Ms. Humphreys looked at her with wide eyes. "All this time, I've been living next door to an angel."

Katrina shook her head and laughed. "That couldn't be further from the truth."

"But you whisked me out without using the door. I saw you wave your hand, and then we were outside, just like that." She imitated the motion Katrina had done. "Only an angel could do that."

"I believe the smoke must be messing with your memory." She walked up the steps to the back door and rammed her shoulder against it, busting it open before gesturing to it. "I'm sorry I had to break your door to get inside."

"That's not…" Confusion furrowed her brow, and a coughing fit racked her body.

"Come." Katrina wrapped an arm around her and guided her around the burning house. "I believe the authorities are here. Let's get you to an ambulance so a doctor can look at you. I'll call your daughter to let her know."

As they rounded the corner and came into view, the crowd watching the scene cheered. Two EMTs approached with a stretcher, and as they loaded Ms. Humphreys onto it, another medical person attempted to guide Katrina to the ambulance.

"I don't require medical attention." She tugged from his grasp. "But I believe the smoke has affected my neighbor's memory of the ordeal."

"She's an angel," Ms. Humphreys said as they loaded her into the ambulance. "She just waved her arm and opened a wormhole to the backyard."

"See what I mean?" After Katrina convinced the EMT she was fine, she searched her contacts for Ms. Humphreys' daughter. She'd gotten the number ages ago after seeing a commercial where an old woman had fallen and couldn't get up. Her neighbor refused to wear the necklace advertised, so Katrina had decided to watch over her.

She filled her daughter in about the ordeal and then answered a billion questions from the fire people until she felt like turning her magic on full-blast and inciting an orgy just so they'd let her go. Seriously, if she'd known the aftermath would be this tedious, she'd have stayed inside with the inferno. She'd rather the building burn to ash around her than endure another minute of their questions.

With the fire under control and the inquisition over, Katrina headed to Jasmine's house. When her BFF answered the door, her brow shot up and her mouth fell open.

"Holy ghost guts! What happened to you?" She grabbed her arm and tugged her inside. Her reaper husband Asher sat lounging on the couch, and he shot to his feet when he saw her.

Katrina crossed her arms. "Why are you both looking at me like I've grown a tail?"

"Have you seen yourself lately?" Asher asked.

Katrina sighed and walked to the mirror hanging above the fireplace. "Oh my." Her face was covered in soot, and ashes matted in her hair. "Aren't I a hot mess… emphasis on the hot?" She smirked and said, "May I use your shower and a change of clothes?"

"Aren't you going to tell us what happened?" Jasmine asked.

"My neighbor set our house on fire. I had to portal into her home to save her, and now she thinks I'm an angel."

Asher laughed.

"I had the same reaction," Katrina said.

"Wow." Jasmine led her down to the hall to the bathroom. "Do you need a place to stay?"

"Do you mind? I don't want to intrude on your sexy times with your man, but I won't be allowed back into my home for at least a day or two, and then I can only see what personal items I can salvage."

"Of course. You can stay with us as long as you need to."

"Just for a few days. I'll book a hotel room as soon as things get settled." She didn't want to intrude any longer than she had to. If there was one thing Katrina refused to be, it was a burden. She'd wrecked enough lives in her days serving Satan.

After she showered and changed into Jasmine's sweatpants and t-shirt, she crashed in the guest bedroom, exhausted. She slept a solid eight hours and woke to find a message from Gabe—AKA Rene—waiting for her.

It read, *"Good morning. How was the rest of your evening?"*

She smiled in spite of herself, unable to recall a time when anyone other than Jasmine had inquired about her day. She replied, *"My neighbor set my house on fire, and now she thinks I'm an angel because I rescued her."*

She expected his reply to be the cry-laughing emoji with some retort about how wrong the woman was. His actual message caught her off guard, *"Are you okay? Do you need anything?"*

Was that fluttering in her stomach…? Surely not. She cleared her throat and swallowed, but the sensation didn't go away. Instead, her abdomen tightened. She rolled onto her back and held the phone to her chest, staring at the ceiling as she contemplated how to answer.

Could he be sincere, or was this just a ploy to worm his way into her psyche to convince her to change her app? At this point, it could be either, but she couldn't deny she enjoyed the initial sensation of butterflies in her belly.

Oh, get over yourself, woman. He's an incubus. Of course he's trying to worm his way in. Because wasn't that exactly what she was doing to him? A pang of something unpleasant flashed in her chest, which was odd as all getout. Could that be guilt? Demons weren't supposed to feel guilt.

If her plan worked, and he fell in love with her, she would end up hurting him in the end. But he'd hurt her first by barging into her town and stealing her business, so they'd be even.

She replied, *"I'm fine. Staying with a friend until I can book a hotel."*

Swinging her legs over the side of the bed, she sat up and set her phone on the nightstand. There was that sinking, nauseating feeling again. How strange.

Her phone buzzed with another message: *"I hear the Bellevue Manor B and B is nice."*

Now there was an idea…

CHAPTER NINE

K atrina sat in Mike's restaurant, Honoré's, nibbling on a slice of garlic bread as she waited for Antoine to arrive for their lunch meeting. She'd snagged a table in a quiet back room of the Magazine Street Victorian mansion, and she lifted her gaze from her current read as a server refilled her sweet tea.

The room was quaint, with wooden tables and mismatched chairs that looked like they came from a dozen different grandmas' houses, and the scent of Cajun spices danced in the air.

She'd postponed the meeting by two days so she could check on Ms. Humphreys, who was out of the hospital and staying with her daughter, and deal with the horrid insurance adjusters and contractors. Of course the adjuster didn't want to give her the full amount required to make the repairs—they rarely did—but a little pulse of demon magic was all it took for Katrina to get everything she needed for both herself and Ms. Humphreys. It was no wonder Satan had a special place in hell reserved for the dishonest people in that profession.

She had also put off getting a room at the B and B. Jasmine and Asher didn't seem to mind her company, but that was because of what she was doing for them. She grinned at the thought. They'd had the best sex of their lives the past two nights since Katrina's magic worked through walls. The mornings after she'd gifted them with the stamina of the Energizer Bunny—they'd kept going and going—they'd stumbled out for breakfast looking fully satiated and more in love than she'd ever seen them. Jasmine had tilted her head, Katrina had given her a wink, and she'd mouthed the words *thank you.*

But she didn't want to wear out her welcome, so tonight, she would move to Bellevue Manor until her home was repaired. Okay, maybe she had put off the move for one other reason. She wasn't quite ready to play out the forced proximity trope she'd learned about in her research. Apparently, when two people who were attracted to each other were forced to stay in the same building, they would fall in love and live happily ever after. It was even better if they were forced to stay in the same room with only one bed, but *that* would not be happening.

Her phone buzzed on the table, and her heart did a weird *beat…beat, beat, beat* thing. It had been happening every time a notification came through for the past two days, and she wasn't sure what it meant. The message was most likely Antoine apologizing for being late, so there was no reason for the strange flush of adrenaline running through her veins.

She picked up the phone and found a message from Gabe. Now her pulse sprinted, and her lips curved into a smile, which had been happening a lot lately too. She would have to discuss these strange sensations with Jasmine. She'd never felt them before.

"Good afternoon. How's your day going?"

Her smile widened. These little check-ins came a couple of times a day, and each time she received one, her stomach fluttered. Surely he was busy with his lectures and coaching and whatever the hell else he was doing, yet he took time out of his day to chat with her.

She replied, *"Good. I'm about to meet with my app developer to make some improvements to Swipe Right."*

"Finally adding that bio section?" He ended the sentence with a winking emoji.

"Perhaps. I have to do something to combat the new demon who swept into town, intent on destroying me." She bit her lip, hesitating to hit send. Her thumb hovered over the button. She hadn't talked to him about this subject yet. Subtle flirting had been her MO for the past couple of days, and she wasn't sure she wanted to change her plan of attack.

"Hey. Sorry I'm late." Antoine's voice startled her, and her hand jerked, her thumb hitting Send. *Whoops.* It looked like her MO was changing.

She turned her phone face down on the table and flagged over the server. "You usually are. Let's order. I'm starving."

When the server arrived, Katrina asked for the roast beef po-boy with extra debris. The little bits of meat that fell off the roast when they cooked it and simmered in the bottom of the stew were her absolute favorite. Antoine got the fried crawfish and then excused himself to the restroom. As he walked away, Katrina's phone buzzed, and her pulse rate kicked up again. She hesitated to turn it over. Maybe she should just leave it until her meeting was done, but the anticipation made her knee bounce incessantly beneath the table. What was up with her body lately?

She picked up her phone and read his reply: *"Uh oh. What makes you think he's trying to sabotage you?"*

Oh, we're going there, are we? She typed her response, *"He came into my town teaching these lessons to supes that completely go against everything my app is about. He's stealing my customers, and frankly, I'm surprised you chose my app over his classes. You seem like you'd be a good fit for him."* She hit send before she could second-guess herself and silenced the notifications on her phone.

"What are you smiling about?" Antoine sank into his chair. His curly black hair was sheared short to his head, and his dark brown eyes held a questioning look.

Katrina shrugged. "Nothing important. Did you get the new retention screen working yet?"

"Yep. It's ready to go live as soon as you approve it." He slid his phone toward her and walked her through the extra *are you sure?* steps the new cancellations would have to go through. He'd bolded, centered, and italicized the large font warning them every potential match would be lost forever if they canceled.

"This is good. Yes. Make it go live ASAP." She reached for her phone but jerked her hand away. This was a working lunch. She would deal with Gabe's reaction to her accusation later.

Their food arrived, and as Katrina bit into her sandwich, bits of chopped beef rained down onto her plate. The savory concoction of gravy and slow-roasted meat melted on her tongue, and her body shuddered. "Mmm… Mike makes the best po-boys. It's like an orgasm for my taste buds with every bite."

Antoine gripped the sides of the table, the tendons in

his neck protruding as he tensed. "You need to rein in your demon quick, Katrina. You promised you wouldn't do this to me again."

"Oopsie." Poor guy. He didn't even like women, but he couldn't resist a succubus's magic. No one could. She reset her guise. "Better?"

"Much." He glared at her as he shoved a forkful of crawfish into his mouth.

The server stopped by their table to refill their sweet tea. "How is everything?"

"It's fabulous, hon, but I think I'm going to need a slice of that angel food cake sooner rather than later." She winked. "Mike's po-boys do this to me every time."

The server laughed. "No problem."

Antoine cleared his throat and straightened in his seat. "Everything else is running smoothly. Hopefully the new retention screen will do the trick."

Katrina tapped a finger against her lips. "I wonder if there's something else we can do. What if we added a bio section so people can tell a little bit about themselves?"

Antoine gave her a skeptical look. "I thought you were dead set against bios. I remember you calling them cliché and overdone."

"Yes, that's true. What about a questionnaire? Could we develop a list of personality questions people could answer, and then we could find matches based on that?"

He furrowed his brow and narrowed his dark eyes like he couldn't believe what she had just said. "Are you insane? That goes against everything you told me this app needed to be about."

She lifted her hands and dropped them on the table, shaking her head exasperatedly. "We have to do something to combat these emotional intimacy classes."

"I thought your plan was to take this guy down and send him packing, not 'coexist' like a cheesy bumper sticker." He made air quotes.

Katrina closed her eyes and rubbed her forehead. Antoine was right. Gabe had wormed his way into her psyche and made her question herself, just like he'd planned. She'd let her guard down, allowing his fake concern to make her feel things, and it was time she womaned up.

"Don't listen to me. That was a stupid idea. I have no idea where it came from. The new retention screen is all we need. You're absolutely right."

"I'm not trying to tell you how to run your business or anything. But you did say—"

She held up a hand. "It was a much-needed reminder. Thank you for keeping me on track, Antoine."

He grinned. "Does this mean I get a raise?"

"If you can keep people from canceling their accounts, I will consider it."

Gabe sat at a small pink table inside Sweet Destiny's Bakery and stared at his phone. He'd stopped in for a slice of angel food cake to prepare himself for tonight's HA meeting. It had been a full week since he'd seen Katrina, but they'd messaged so much he felt like he was getting to know her. She had a brilliant mind. She was confident and a little sassy. Intriguing, to say the least.

He ran his fork through the strawberry sauce on his plate and sank it into the cake. Half an hour had passed since the last message he sent, and Katrina had yet to reply. He shoveled the cake into his mouth and reread his text for the umpteenth time.

"I've heard of the classes, but your app seemed like it would be easier than trying to meet people out in the wild. Have you ever considered that he didn't know about you or your app when he came to New Orleans? Have you tried talking to him about it? Surely there's a way you can get along."

His patience was running thin. Too many days had passed without much progress in Project Make Katrina Fall in Love. She'd liked his suggestion of moving into Bellevue Manor while her home was under repair, yet she was still staying with her friend. Tonight might be his only chance to make a connection with her in person. If she would just reply to his message and continue the conversation, he could warm her up to the idea of a dinner date… or at least a civil conversation.

Destiny, the bakery's namesake angel, glided into the dining area from behind the counter. Her copper hair flowed past her shoulders, and she wore a white sundress with gold sandals. "What problem are you facing, Gabe?" Her voice was smooth and soothing, and she smiled sweetly.

"What makes you think I have a problem?" He went for another bite of cake, but he'd already finished it.

She stood by his table and clasped her hands. "Demons don't dine in unless their souls are troubled. My magic soothes the beast inside you *and* your heart. What brought you in?"

He checked his phone again. Katrina hadn't replied. "I don't suppose you could bake a love spell into one of your cakes, could you?"

She tilted her head. "I believe you know that's not how angels work."

"It was worth a shot." He drummed his fingers on the table.

"Give it time. If it's meant to be, they'll return your affections eventually."

And there was the problem. He wasn't trying to get Katrina to *return* his affections; he was trying to make the love a one-sided deal. "I've only got two more weeks."

Her face pinched. "Have you bargained with…Satan?" She whispered the bastard's name as if she were afraid she'd accidentally summon him.

He nodded slowly. "Yep."

"Oh, dear. Hearts should never be bargained with. What will you lose if the match can't be made?"

He inhaled deeply before releasing an abrupt puff of air. "The rest of my manhood."

She drew her lips inward and lifted her brow. "I'm afraid you'll lose far more than that if you fail. Who are you trying to woo?"

"Katrina Alarie."

She let out a low whistle.

"Tell me about it."

"Deceit is detrimental to a recovering demon. You need to be honest, or you will never succeed."

Honest? Yeah, right. Even if the contract allowed him to tell her, he could imagine how that conversation would go. *Hey, Katrina. The Devil will grant you your freedom if you fall in love with the man you hate the most, so could we skip the courtship and head right to marriage?* Sure, she'd go for that.

A notification buzzed, and his heart sprinted. "Thanks

for the advice, but she can't know what's happening." He grabbed the phone and swiped open the screen.

"I meant be honest with yourself." Destiny took his empty plate and returned to the kitchen.

He held his breath as he read Katrina's message: *"I have come to believe he didn't know what he was doing when he arrived. We spoke about it once, but the conversation didn't go well."*

"Maybe you should try again." He held his breath as the annoying dots bounced on the screen. Then they stopped, and his body tensed until her reply finally came through.

"I'm not sure he would forgive me. I was rather wicked to him when I thought he was working for Satan."

He would forgive her. How could he not? *"It never hurts to try."*

"Perhaps, but enough about my dilemma. Tell me, Rene, how is your day going?"

Gabe smiled. She seemed to be growing fond of his Rene persona. Now if he could figure out a way to have her grow fond of the real man behind the mask.

CHAPTER TEN

Katrina sat in her place in the "Circle of Hope," greeting the other demons as they entered the room. With her legs crossed, she wiggled her foot in what could only be anticipation, which was downright ridiculous. It had been a full week since she'd seen Gabe, but she'd messaged with him so much she felt as if they were becoming friends.

That was also utterly ridiculous. Making a new friend would indicate she was friendly—a personality trait she simply did not possess. Yet, a strange nervousness rolled through her stomach just the same. She would have to discuss these unfamiliar emotions with Jasmine to figure them out. They made no sense to her.

It was possible she'd read too many romance novels and her mind was fabricating the sensations. Yes, that was it. Nervous anticipation was a common feeling amongst the heroines of the stories when they were about to see their hero.

Gabe was not her hero. Far from it. She was on a mission to sabotage his business, to get him wrapped around her finger so she could break his heart and send him packing. Why was it so hard for her to remember that?

Richard entered the room and scratched his massive belly as he gave her a funny look.

"Good evening." She nodded a hello, and he shook his head before heading straight to the snack table and gorging on the plate of pralines she'd picked up from the bakery down the road. The famine demon had done a complete one-eighty with his life, thanks to the Hellions Anonymous meetings keeping him on track. Even Sarah had no problem masking up these days to keep from perpetuating the pandemic.

Katrina gazed at the ceiling before taking in the rest of the drab room. The fluorescent lights cast a greenish tinge in the space, and brown stains spread across several of the ceiling tiles. The once-white walls now had a beige tint with peeling paint in the corners. Perhaps it was time she found a more appealing meeting space. Her HA members deserved better.

"Are you okay?" Mike's deep voice drew her from her thoughts.

"Of course. Why wouldn't I be?" She clasped her hands on her knee.

"You're smiling, for one." He gestured to her wiggling foot. "And you look like you're ready to race a speed demon."

She uncrossed her legs and placed her feet side by side on the floor. "I have a new trust experiment planned for us after the required introductions, and I'm excited to get started." That wasn't a complete lie. She did research team-building exercises before the meeting to find something to get her closer to Gabe. Making bodily contact with a man who preached emotions first would be next to impossible without a carefully orchestrated plan.

But her smile and her wiggling foot…those were complications from reading the romance novels. Succubi did not feel any emotions that weren't diabolical or horny as hell. And speaking of horny…

Gabe walked into the room, wearing dark jeans that hugged his muscular thighs and a gray t-shirt that showed off his pecs and biceps. *Yum.* He must have been one helluva sex demon before he won his freedom. Even with his guise fully intact, Katrina's mouth watered at the sight of him.

He made eye contact, and his irises flashed red before he looked away. Katrina's own eyes heated, which meant hers were red too, which also meant her guise was slipping. How could it not with that much hotness in the room?

"Eat up." Mike shoved a plate toward her, and she pushed it away.

"I'm not hungry." Not for food anyway. She could, however, make a meal out of Gabriel Dakota.

Mike grabbed her hand and placed the plate in her grip. "Eat it anyway. You need it."

"Please, Katrina?" Sarah rubbed a hand on her own thigh before clutching her knee in a death grip. "I'm really not in the mood for a demon orgy."

Katrina swept her gaze across the other demons in the circle. *Whoops.* After an impromptu HA sex-fest a decade or so ago, she'd made a promise to them all that she would never unleash her magic at the meetings. She shoved the entire mini angel food cake into her mouth. "Sorry," she mumbled around the pastry.

Gabe took a cake for himself and sat directly across

from her in the circle. "Is my being here going to be a problem? I'm sure I could find another meeting a town over. Does Metairie have an HA group?"

Katrina straightened her spine and crossed her legs. "It's no problem at all. You are perfectly welcome here."

"He is?" Richard asked. "That's not what you said—"

"Of course he is." She cut him a look that could turn lava into ice. "All hellions are welcome at my meetings." She turned to Gabe, whose gaze had dropped to her bare calf. "It's good to see you again."

He looked into her eyes. "Is it?"

She raised her hands and then dropped them in her lap. "Would you all stop questioning me? Gabe is as welcome as any of us. Now, let's begin. Hi, I'm Katrina, and I'm a succubus."

"Hi, Katrina," they said in unison…all except for Gabe, who arched a brow and spoke after the others, "Hello, Katrina."

His deep, smooth voice wrapped around her like satin sheets fresh from the wash, making her shiver. From the look on his face, it must've been a visible tremor. She cleared her throat and told her story.

They went around the circle, as usual, and when it was Gabe's turn, he shared the bare minimum again. "I fell in love with a human, and when Satan wanted me to ruin him, I bargained for my freedom."

That wasn't good enough. She needed to get him to open up and share more if she was ever going to penetrate his defenses. "Will you tell us what happened to your human?"

Gabe clenched his jaw. "He's dead."

"How did he die?" She asked in the sweetest voice she could muster.

He inhaled deeply before letting his breath out slowly, hesitating as he looked into her eyes. His lips formed a thin line as he pressed them together, and as she held his gaze, something strange happened. The rest of the room ceased to exist; they were the only two people there.

Of course, that didn't *really* happen. All the other demons sat in the circle, waiting for his answer, but the sensation that she and Gabe were the only demons in the world happened, just like in the books she read. Her pulse even began to sprint.

Gabe nodded once and spoke, "Satan first sent another incubus, but Jason was immune to his power. Then he sent a succubus. When she couldn't seduce him, he sent a trooper demon to destroy him the old-fashioned way."

"That sucks, man," Mike said. "I'm sorry that happened."

"It was decades ago." His gaze didn't stray from Katrina's eyes, and another foreign sensation expanded in her chest.

She thought back to the second or third novel she'd read and how the heroine felt when she thought the hero had died in the fire. She couldn't recall the title, but the way that book had described the emotions…Katrina could almost feel them herself, and they were devastating.

"I'm so sorry." The words didn't even register in her brain before they escaped her lips.

"Thank you," he said before clearing his throat and clapping Richard on the shoulder. "Your turn."

Okay, that was weird. Those books had poisoned her mind. It was the only explanation for the strange sensations stirring inside her. Unless a demon was half-human like Mike, they weren't capable of the full range of human emotions. Her mind was fabricating these weaknesses, and it was time she took back control.

Operation flirtation was now in full swing.

After the rest of the demons introduced themselves, Katrina rose to her feet. "We all know part of the required curriculum is team-building exercises."

A collective groan emanated from the demons.

"Hey, I don't make the rules, but we do have to follow them if we want to continue living topside." She crossed her arms, shifting her weight to her right leg. "Unless you all want to return to hell?"

The demons grumbled, but they reluctantly stood. Gabe had an interesting smirk on his face like he was fighting a smile. What could that be about? He'd probably thought of another way for "Rene" to manipulate her into changing her app. *Typical demon.*

"Okay, I need everyone to stand in a tight circle." She motioned with her hands, and the demons scooted inward. "It needs to be *really tight.*" She winked at Gabe as she emphasized the last two words, and he had to try even harder to fight his smile.

"I hope this isn't going to be *too hard.*" One corner of his mouth lifted with his brow.

"There is no such thing." She slipped out her tongue to moisten her lips, and his gaze followed. *Game on.*

Mike cleared his throat, pulling her attention from Gabe, and she found every demon in the circle staring at her in disbelief. Honestly, she was a succubus. Did they really expect her not to flirt with her immortal enemy? Sex was her greatest weapon.

"Tighter, y'all. Shoulder to shoulder." She tapped a few of them on the backs, getting them to scoot closer. "No one's going to bite."

"Speak for yourself," Thom, a gluttony demon said.

Katrina shook her head. "No biting. Now, everyone turn to their right." They all turned. "Your other right, Richard."

"Sorry." He spun in the correct direction.

"Scoot in closer. We need to be almost heel to toe." She went around the circle, ushering everyone inward until they looked like the instructional video she'd watched. "On the count of three, we're all going to sit down at once."

"Oh, hell no." Mindy, a petite demon who stood behind Richard, stepped out of the circle. "He'll crush me."

"We'll all crush each other," Sarah said.

"No, we won't," Katrina assured them. "Our weight will be evenly distributed if we all sit at the same time."

"Have you tried this before?" Mike asked.

"No, but the YouTube video I watched explained it all. It will work." The demons shook their heads skeptically, and Katrina sighed. "Mike, please stand behind Richard. I'm sure you can hold his weight."

Mike did as he was asked, and Mindy stood behind him while Gabe watched Katrina with an amused expression. If only she had mind-reading abilities. Wait... Why did she care what he was thinking? She shouldn't... She didn't. No, she should because she was on a mission to make him want her. *Gah!* This was so confusing.

"Everyone, put your hands on the shoulders of the person in front of you. I'm just going to wiggle in here." She shimmied in between Gabe and the woman in front of him. His hands felt nice on her shoulders, warm and strong, and his chuckle sent a tingle down her spine. *Very confusing.*

"Ready to sit? One, two, three!"

Everyone sat, and praise the Devil, it worked! No, not praise the Devil. Satan had nothing to do with this. Praise…*something*. Anyway, she was sitting in Gabe's lap, exactly where she wanted to be.

She leaned her head back. "Are you doing okay back there?"

"Never better." His lips didn't quite brush her ear as he spoke, but the movement of his mouth rustled her hair, making a delightful sensation warm in her chest. Odd. Most of the pleasurable feelings she experienced happened down under, which was where his should have been happening too. It was time to cause some friction on his dicktion.

"Now we're going to walk."

"Are you crazy?" Mindy shouted.

"We'll all start on the right. One, two, three." She moved her foot forward, and thankfully so did everyone else. "Now left." The demon's ass in her lap moved from side to side, and if Katrina had a cock, it would have been rock hard with the rubbing.

Gabe's, however, was not.

"Faster!" she called, and they picked up the pace. How in Satan's realm was Gabe's heat-seeking moisture missile not locked and loaded? Any man, even Satan himself, would be as hard as a crowbar with a succubus in his lap, so how was he resisting her?

"Teamwork, y'all. Faster, faster! See what we can accomplish when we *come* together?"

Gabe laughed, but she didn't get a rise out of him. *How on Earth?*

They kept it up, moving faster in a circle until Richard tripped the demon in front of him. His foot caught the other man's, and they tumbled inward, creating a domino of demons. Butts smacked tile, and arms flailed as grunts and groans filled the air.

"Ow! Get off me." Mindy scrambled from beneath Mike, and the other demons followed suit, clambering to their feet and dusting off their clothes.

Katrina rose to her knees and looked at Gabe, who sat, grinning, on the floor. "Everyone *got up* but you."

"I guess they did." He laughed and stood before offering her a hand up.

She accepted—the more physical contact, the better— and addressed the group. "I think that's enough team building for today. Have a good night, everyone."

Katrina had a new dilemma to address. How the hell was she going to get Gabe wrapped around her finger if she couldn't charm his pants snake into standing at attention?

The demons filed out of the meeting room, Richard taking the leftover snacks, as usual, and Sarah stayed behind to help Katrina fold up the chairs. Gabe hovered in the doorway, hesitating to leave, and Katrina leaned over to whisper in Sarah's ear, "I've got this, hon. You head on home."

"Are you sure?"

She looked at Gabe. "Positive."

CHAPTER ELEVEN

Gabe stepped aside as Sarah scurried out the door, leaving him alone with Katrina. The welcome he received when he arrived at the meeting was unexpected, to say the least. Maybe Katrina really did feel bad about the way she'd treated him last week. It was time he found out so he could decide how to proceed with his plans.

"Let me help you." He sauntered into the room and picked up a chair before folding it and setting it against the wall.

"Thank you. Sarah usually stays to help me clean up, but she had to run." She offered him a small smile and continued moving the chairs.

"That was an interesting exercise you had us do. Our group leader in San Francisco never incorporated team building into our meetings. I guess he didn't follow the rules."

She rested a chair against the wall and bit her lip. It wasn't a seductive gesture. She looked almost embarrassed in an adorable way, and Gabe's stomach clenched as an unwelcome emotion expanded in his chest.

"I have a confession." She lifted one shoulder. "Team building exercises aren't required by law. They aren't even suggested."

"Then why do you do them?"

"It helps the demons learn to get along with others. I know they've all bargained for their freedom because they don't want to be evil anymore, but we are all evil at our cores. Working together and having a little fun reminds us why we're topside."

"Evil at your core, yet intent on helping others."

She raised a finger. "Lying to them to do it, though."

He laughed. "You are an interesting character."

She pursed her lips, drawing his attention to the way they resembled a bow. "Please don't tell the others about this. I shouldn't even have told you."

"Why did you?" He folded another chair and rested it against the wall.

"I think I should apologize."

"No need. I won't say a word to the others, so you won't have to apologize for lying."

She picked up the last chair and leaned it on the stack against the wall. "I should apologize to you. I'm sorry for sabotaging your lecture and for being rude at the last meeting. It was no way for a recovering demon to treat one of her own."

He shoved his hands into his pockets, a bit taken aback by her sincerity. He'd expected nothing more than a half-hearted "sorry."

"This is the part where you say I'm forgiven." She brushed her hair behind her shoulder before resting a hand on her hip.

"No worries. I rescheduled the event, and the turnout was even better."

Her jaw clamped shut with an audible *click*.

Good going, dumbass. The way to win the woman's heart is not by rubbing in your own success.

"I should apologize too." He stepped toward her. "I never meant to steal your business. I didn't even know your app was a thing until someone told me at the first lecture."

She crossed her arms, obviously not buying his apology.

He continued, "If I'd known it was you running the service, I wouldn't have suggested they cancel their accounts."

"Oh? And why not?"

"Because that's no way to treat one of my own." He moved closer, and thankfully she didn't back away. "I haven't suggested it since."

"Yet people are *still* canceling in droves."

"There must be some way we can figure out how to coexist." He moved even closer, though why he wasn't sure. Okay, that was bullshit. He knew why; he just didn't want to admit it.

He was attracted to her. Emotionally *and* physically, and he wanted to be near her. Having her in his lap during their team-building exercise had stirred up sensations he hadn't felt in decades. He was an incubus at his heart, sure. He thought about sex more than he wanted to, but that was his nature. With Katrina, it was more than sex on his mind, and that was a problem. In his quest to make her catch feelings for him, he was starting to have them for her. *Fuck me.*

"Have you had dinner?" she asked.

"Umm…" *Answer the woman. This is your chance.*

"I'm starving and thought I'd stop for a bite on my way home. You can join me if you'd like."

"Yeah. I'd like that." She was full of surprises, wasn't she?

She raked her gaze down his form, pausing below the belt before flicking it to his eyes. "I'm in the mood for sausage. Let's go to Dat Dog. If you don't mind dumpsters, there's a secluded spot we can portal to." She held out her hand, and he accepted.

"Sounds good to me."

With her other arm, she sliced open a portal, and they stepped through into an alley. He recognized the sounds of Frenchman street as they made their way toward the main road, and the bright blue two-story with yellow trim and pink wrought iron across the way sported a sign with a cartoon hot dog that read "Dat Dog."

Gabe followed her inside, and they stopped in front of a large menu hanging on the wall. The restaurant offered traditional-style hot dogs as well as more exotic choices like alligator and duck sausage.

Katrina ordered something called The Rougarou, and she turned to Gabe. "What'll you have? My treat since you're new in town."

"The Bacon Werewolf sounds good."

Katrina grinned slyly. "Have you ever had a werewolf?"

He chuckled. "Can't say that I have."

"They're delicious if you don't mind the fleas."

The man at the counter furrowed his brow curiously, and Katrina winked at him before leading Gabe to a table in the back corner. He sat across from her, and she rested her elbow on the table, leaning her chin into the backs of her fingers. Her smile was contagious, and he found himself grinning back at her. Yep. He was in trouble.

"So…does this mean we're friends now?" He fisted his hands in his lap.

"I have another confession." She folded her arms on the table and leaned toward him. "I enjoyed sitting in your lap more than I should have." Her magic buzzed across his skin before he even realized what she was doing. Warm and inviting, it penetrated the surface, resonating in his core like the most exquisite invitation he'd ever received.

He closed his eyes, basking in the erotic electricity she shared with him. It would be the most he could ever experience with her.

"Did you enjoy it, Gabe?" she purred.

Satan's balls, did he ever. But it was time to pull himself out of her trance. "Why the sudden change of heart? You seemed ready to claw my eyes out the last time we were together."

She blinked as if shocked her magic didn't have him naked and drooling at her feet already. Then she reeled it in and composed herself. "I wouldn't say it was sudden. I've been doing a lot of soul-searching over the week, and I decided I was too hard on you."

"I thought you said there was no such thing?"

She made a noncommittal sound. "I feel like we should get acquainted better before we decide how *hard* to be on each other."

"I agree." The tension in his shoulders eased, and he relaxed his hands on his thighs. "Tell me, aside from running your app, what else do you like to do?"

"Oh, I think you know plenty about me. I want to know more about you. Tell me about your deal with Satan. How did you get him to release you?"

"Uh-uh." He shook his head. "That's far too personal to share so soon."

Her lips pouted as she drummed her fingers on the table, but when she opened her mouth to speak again, a server delivered their food.

"Bon appetite." She bit into her hot dog and moaned. "It's so good."

Oh, yeah. She was a succubus, all right. She even ate erotically. *Damn.*

Their conversation over dinner consisted mostly of his thoughts about the city, places he'd been, what he had yet to see. Katrina loved the nightlife, using little bursts of her magic to give people the courage to talk to the ones who caught their eyes. She was in tune with humans way more than any demon he'd ever met, and her fondness of the mortals was an endearing quality.

"It's sweet the way you enjoy helping people." He wiped his mouth with a napkin and pushed his plate aside.

"It's not that I *enjoy* helping them. I'm a sex demon who can't have sex. It's the closest I ever get. Not that I'd expect you to understand."

She would be surprised…

Katrina set her empty plate on top of his and leaned forward. "There might be something *you* could do about that, though." Her magic shimmied over his skin again, and his body shuddered. *If* there were something he could do about it, she wouldn't need to use her powers to get it from him. Even with her guise fully intact, he found her irresistible. Thankfully, his cock was out of commission. Otherwise, he couldn't help but give in to his desires. If they never made it past sex, he'd never break through her walls and convince her she could love.

"Katrina, you have to stop using your magic on me if we're going to be friends. Sex is off the table."

"What about under the table? On the floor in your room?"

He chuckled and shook his head. "It's not going to happen."

"Are you sure? It's what we're both made for." She gave her power another pulse, and if his soldier were capable, it would've been saluting. "I don't see any harm in the two of us having some fun. You're the only man in New Orleans I can't destroy."

He reached across the table to place his hand on hers, and Beelzebub have mercy, he should not have done that. Her magic zipped up his arm, zapped his chest, and played pinball with his organs on its way down to his crotch. His balls tightened in response, but his dick hung limp as a string of yarn. He managed a curt, "No."

"Why not?" She pulled from his grasp, and for the first time since he'd met her, uncertainty creased her brow.

"Because I'm not leaving New Orleans. I'm not going to stop being a relationship coach. If we are going to coexist in the city, we need to be friends. *Just* friends." Yes, that was a lie. He needed her to feel so much more than friendship toward him, but she didn't seem to grasp the concept of romantic love yet.

"Friends with benefits?" She smiled as she reeled in her power, but it didn't mask the hurt in her eyes.

Gods, how he would love to have those benefits. Even with her magic turned off, his mind drifted to all the things he would love to do to her. But he couldn't. And even if he could, he shouldn't. "No benefits. Just friends for now."

"You said 'for now.'" Her tone was playful, adorable. "That means we could have benefits in the future."

He closed his eyes and let out a slow breath. If he could pull this off, maybe they could.

"You didn't say no," she sang.

He chuckled. "How about we get to know each other better? You haven't told me much about you."

"Okay, I suppose that'll do for now." Her smile widened. "But excuse me for one second. I need to check in with someone before we begin." She pulled out her phone and typed on the screen.

Gabe's phone buzzed in his pocket, and his gaze snapped to hers. She winked, lifting one brow seductively, and he tugged the device from his pocket to find a message from her.

Hello, Rene. How did you enjoy your bacon werewolf?

Busted. Honestly, he shouldn't have been surprised. Katrina was as sharp as Satan's pitchfork. He returned his phone to his pocket and clasped his hands on the table. "When did you figure it out?"

"The moment we started messaging. You're a horrible liar, even through the most easy-to-lie-on medium."

That was something he'd never been called before. Demons were masterful liars. "How long were you planning to string me along, pretending you didn't know it was me?"

"String you—?" She scoffed. "You're the one who started it. I should be asking you the same question. What was your purpose for trying to fool me?"

Whoops. He'd struck a nerve. Time for damage control. "I'm sorry, Katrina. It was a stupid move, and I should have been honest with you."

She crossed her arms. "You didn't answer my question."

He nodded, lifting his shoulders and dropping them

hard. "I suppose I was trying to...soften you up. Our last in-person conversation proved you'd pegged me as your enemy, and I thought if you got to know me, you might be willing to talk to me. Maybe even collaborate."

"Collaborate..." She shook her head in disbelief. "You've been trying to manipulate me. To get me to change the purpose of my app. What was your end game, Gabe? To take it over? To shut it down? You *are* trying to sabotage me."

"No. No, Katrina, I promise I'm not. I really do want to be friends. We're not so different, you and me. We could find a way to meet in the middle."

She stood and fisted her hands at her sides. "We are far too much at odds for that. The only middle I'm willing to meet you in is the middle of a mattress, but you've made it clear you don't find me attractive." She gasped when the words left her mouth, pressing her hand to her chest like she couldn't believe she'd said them.

"Katrina, I do find you attractive." And the more he got to know her, the more attractive she became.

"Well, you've got a fucked-up way of showing it. If you don't want to do the pants-off dance-off, you're of no use to me. Goodbye." She turned on her heel and marched out of the restaurant.

"Katrina, wait." He darted after her, following her into the alley, but she ducked behind the dumpster and portaled away.

CHAPTER TWELVE

Her portal should have worked. She could see her destination on the other side of the opening, so when she stepped through, she should have been alone in her rented room to lick her wounds and figure out what the hell was happening inside her body.

Instead, she smacked into the white wood siding with a *thwack*, bounced off, and landed flat on her back in the B and B's courtyard. "Holy fucking hellhounds. What the hell, man?" She sat up and rubbed the back of her head. That was sure to leave a bruise.

Gaston, who sat on the back porch sipping blood from a crystal glass, winced. "Oh, dear. It seems my day help didn't tell you about the portal-proof forcefield when you checked in."

"No, he did not." She rose to her feet and dusted the grass from her skirt. "Why don't you fill me in?"

"My apologies." He steepled his fingers. "I do hope this won't negatively influence your Haunt Ads review. I have a five-star average, and I'd like to keep it that way."

She dragged a wrought iron chair across the wooden

deck and plopped into it. "Why can't I portal into my room?"

"I employed Crimson, the high priestess, to cast a spell to protect the mansion from all portals. I can't have demons popping in and using my facilities without a reservation."

"But I *do* have a reservation. I'm going to be here for a long time, thanks to my senile neighbor. Can't you rig it so your paying guests can portal in?"

He rubbed his thumb and forefinger on his chin. "I'm not sure that's possible, but I will look into it. Do you think it would improve customer satisfaction?"

"Yes, dear. It would." She smirked and rose to her feet. "Is the courtyard at least secluded enough?"

He nodded. "Feel free to portal away, but you'll need your key card to enter the building."

"Noted." She paced to the door, pressed her damn card against the unlocking mechanism, and stepped inside.

Her hands trembled as she made her way up the stairs, so she curled them into fists. Her stomach churned, the sour sensation rising to her chest and making it burn. Funny, she'd never gotten heartburn from a hot dog before.

She made a sharp left at the top of the stairs and froze. Gabe stood in the hallway, unlocking the door a few feet from hers. *Fan-fucking-tastic.* They were neighbors. He opened his mouth as if to speak, so she raised a hand and shook her head before making a beeline for her room.

Her palms slickened, and her key card slipped from her grasp before she could unlock her door. "Fuck!" She picked it up and dropped it again while Gabe stood there watching her. She finally grabbed the slippery sucker and pressed it to the lock before snapping her gaze to the infuriating demon.

"I'm here when you're ready to talk." He had a strange look in his eyes. One she couldn't begin to decipher with her thoughts running a mile a minute.

"Fuck off." She stepped into her room and slammed the door.

With her back against the wood, she slid to the floor, stretching out her legs in a narrow V and leaning her head back. "What the ever-loving hell is happening to me?"

Her stomach grew even more sour, her chest burning like a lava pit in hell. This was not heartburn. Was it heartache? No, her heart wasn't capable of such pain. It was some new form of anger. It had to be.

Gabe had rejected her. *Rejected* her. No man, incubus or otherwise, had ever been able to resist her magic…not even Satan himself. But Gabe did. He didn't want her. How was that possible?

The burning in her chest morphed into a strange sort of ache. She'd never been rejected before. Was this what all those poor people without her magic felt like when their affections weren't returned?

Affections. *Ha!* She held no affinity for Gabe. If she had any of those pesky emotions at all, they were for "Rene," not the real person. She could admit his fake persona had provided her a sense of comfort she'd never experienced before. Perhaps she had grown fond of the faux interest he'd shown in her, but it was all a scam. She'd known what he was doing from the beginning, yet she'd let him get to her. She'd allowed herself, if only for a moment, to imagine she was the heroine in one of Jasmine's novels, and now a slew of weird, unwelcome emotions undulated in her gut. She had to get rid of them.

She sliced open a portal, intent on heading to her bestie's house, but the moment she stepped through, she bounced off the wall and landed flat on her ass in her own room. "Fuck Gaston and his stupid portal-proof mansion. Ugh!"

Katrina scrambled to her feet, dusted off her wounded pride, and cracked open the door. Living next to her nemesis was the last thing she wanted to do now, but she'd booked Gaston's last room. She couldn't move to the third floor, so she was stuck.

Peeking down the hall, she found Gabe's door closed, so she tip-toed toward the staircase. Light spilled out beneath the threshold, and she was tempted to bang on the door and give him a piece of her mind. Though, she wasn't sure what she would even say to him. She didn't understand what she was feeling herself.

She held her breath as she passed his room and then darted down the stairs and out the back door. The air from her lungs came out in a rush of relief as she made it to the porch. What in Satan's realm was wrong with her? She needed advice, and she needed it now.

When she swiped open another portal, she hesitated to step through. She'd already been slammed against a wall twice this evening—and not in the fun kind of way—but Gaston had assured her it was safe to portal from the courtyard, so she hopped into Jasmine's living room.

"Hey, Jazz, I need your help." She glanced around the room. A single lamp on the end table illuminated the space, and the smell of lavender and smoke from half a dozen extinguished candles drifted in the air. "Jasmine?"

She started toward the hall, but she tripped over a pile of clothes on the floor. Jasmine's clothes. And lying next to them was a massive piece of black fabric. She picked up the heavy garment to examine it. Was this Asher's reaper robe?

She held in a giggle. It seemed her necromancer BFF was raising hell with Death tonight. A feminine moan emanating from the direction of their bedroom confirmed her suspicion. Far be it from a succubus to interrupt her only friend when she was getting boned.

It was just as well. Katrina was a grown-ass demon. She should be able to sort through her emotions on her own. After grabbing another novel from the bookshelf and portaling to the courtyard, she made her way to the second floor as stealthily as possible, but Gabe must've heard her because he opened the door the moment she reached the hallway.

His eyes widened like he was startled, but instead of retreating to his room like a good little demon, he entered the hall and closed the door behind him. "I'm heading down to the sitting room for a drink. Why don't you join me?"

She wanted to scream like a banshee. Why was he tormenting her like this? She managed to growl a "No, thank you" before brushing past him and slipping into her room. *The nerve of that man!*

A steaming hot shower calmed her nerves, and after slipping into her new silk pajamas, she snuggled under the covers and cracked open the book. These damn things were the root of her problems, but she couldn't get enough of them. She told herself she was doing research, looking for a solution to her predicament as she scanned the pages, absorbing the story. But honestly…?

Katrina wanted what these heroines had. It was no secret she wanted to experience love; she admitted it every time she introduced herself at the HA meetings. Reading these novels only reinforced her desire to win her freedom from Satan's control. It was the only way she'd be free to love.

Maybe it was time she paid the Prince of Hell another visit. There was no time like the present, but she hesitated to go. It had been more than a century since she'd ventured to the bowels of hell…a place she had sworn she would never go again.

But this was an emergency. She couldn't tell if she wanted to vomit, scream, or do both at the same time, thanks to all these bizarre sensations swirling inside her. Winning her freedom was the only way she could sort it all out.

But Gabe was downstairs, damn it. She had to get outside without another confrontation. Surely a place like this had an old servants' staircase. It most likely led to the kitchen, which was on the left side of the house, so she padded down the hall, past Gabe's room, and hung a right. Sure enough, she found the stairs hidden behind a narrow wooden door. Adrenaline made her stomach clench and her blood feel electrified as she slipped inside and descended to the kitchen.

But the door that should have led her out was bolted shut. *Fuck me.* That left the back door and the front door as her only means of escape, and she couldn't get to either of those without passing by the living room. She tip-toed across the kitchen and peeked around the corner to find the space empty. Leaning farther into the room to get a better look, she swept her gaze right and left. No Gabe.

"Thank my lucky hunk of brimstone." She scurried across the room and darted out the back door.

Safely outside, she portaled into hell's demon entrance and cringed at the crooning voice piping through the speakers. Christmas music in August? Satan was upping his game in the torture department.

She made her way over the rocky path toward the palace, cursing herself for not rethinking her outfit. Her bare feet would be covered in soot by the time she made it back to her room. She crossed the bridge over the fiery moat and pressed her hand against the metal plate by the door. The moment the massive gate swung open, she marched her perturbed and utterly confused ass straight to Satan's office.

"Hey! You can't go in there!" a woman shouted as she pushed open the door.

"Watch me." Katrina strode toward Satan's desk and found him playing with a fluffy white cat. He held a stick with a feathery ball hanging from it over the feline, who batted at it with its paw.

"Satan, I've had enough." She stopped in front of his desk and crossed her arms.

His brow shot up, and he dropped the cat toy. "Katrina?" He shooed the feline from his desk and composed himself, turning on his devilish charm. "Silk. You know it's my favorite on you."

Yeah, she really should have rethought her outfit for this excursion. Pajamas were not the way to go. "I can't do this anymore."

He let his gaze wander down her form and sighed. "I appreciate your forwardness and your confidence, love, but I'm back with the banshee for now. She doesn't like to share."

"The screamer? Seriously?"

He shrugged. "I like to torture myself sometimes."

She rolled her eyes. "I'm not here for sex. I want my freedom. Make me a deal."

He had the gall to laugh at her. "Oh, Katrina. Katrina, Katrina, my favorite succubus. I'm afraid I don't want to let you go."

"Please. There has to be something I can do."

"I assume you've met Gabriel?"

"He has nothing to do with this." Her jaw clenched. "Unless you sent him to sabotage me."

He laughed harder. "I assure you I did not, but this is a fun twist. An incubus and a succubus going head-to-head for control of New Orleans."

"How did you know I live in New Orleans?"

"I know everything about you, love. More than you know yourself, it appears. Did you think you were hiding from me?"

She narrowed her eyes. "No." *Yes. Gah!* She was an idiot. If the Devil wouldn't throw her in the tarpits, she'd love to slap that shit-eating grin off his face. "Why won't you make me a deal?"

"Because I enjoy torturing you." He shrugged. "It's as simple as that."

"You're still mad I wouldn't be your girlfriend."

"Nooo…" He waved his hand dismissively. "Satan never holds a grudge. Now, on your way. I've got pressing matters to attend to." He picked up the feather toy, and the cat jumped onto his desk.

"Fuck me."

"Someday soon, love," Satan said as she marched out of his office.

Those were not tears gathering in her eyes. Succubi did not cry. It was the sharp scent of sulfur and the extreme humidity making her eyes water. That was all.

CHAPTER THIRTEEN

"You've ruined me. Your stupid books have ruined me!" Katrina dropped the stack of novels on Jasmine's coffee table and plopped onto the couch. Was she being overly dramatic? Yes. Yes, she was, but she couldn't help it. She didn't understand what was going on inside her, couldn't make sense of all the emotions, couldn't tell if they were real or fabrications of her mind. She felt out of control, and Katrina was *always* in control.

Jasmine whisked the stack away, no doubt afraid Katrina would tear into them like she did Gabe's flyers at the bar. Gabe... *Ugh!*

"I know better than to tell a demon to calm down, but you're going to have to talk to me. What's going on?"

Katrina inhaled deeply, trying to calm the tornado raging in her gut, her chest, her head...hell, *she* was the tornado. "I read those books for research. To learn ways to entice Gabe to have feelings for me so I could manipulate him."

Jasmine sank into the accent chair. "And I take it your plan didn't work?"

"No, it didn't work!" She shot to her feet and paced the length of the room. "He rejected me, Jasmine. I offered myself to him, and he turned me down! He didn't catch feelings, but *I* did." She stopped and shook her hands in the air. "Why is this happening to me?"

"Umm…" Jasmine appeared to be fighting a grin, though what could possibly be funny about this situation, Katrina had no idea. "How many books did you read?"

"I don't know. Twenty or thirty." She plopped onto the couch and rubbed her forehead. "I'm a fast reader. Was that too many?"

Jasmine's mouth formed a bunch of different letters before she finally spoke. "Can we back it up a bit? What kind of feelings do you think you've caught?"

"I don't know! That's the problem. There's all this nausea and fluttering and flitting. Sometimes I smile for no reason, but then I think about him rejecting me and pain expands in my chest. There are far too many physical sensations going on for me to make sense of anything."

Her bestie quit fighting her smile. "You like him."

"I'd love to fuck him six ways to Sunday, but he made it clear he didn't want me."

Now she laughed. "You like *him*, Katrina. You don't just want to sleep with him. You want to spend time with him."

"I don't like the accusation in your tone."

"Let me break it down for you, although, if you've read thirty romance novels, I'd think you'd be able to figure it out."

Katrina narrowed her eyes. "I'm a succubus. We don't know anything about romance."

Jasmine nodded, and amusement danced in her dark brown eyes. "The fluttering and flitting? Even some of the nausea…that happens when you think about him and also when he texts you."

She cast her gaze to the ceiling as she contemplated her friend's statement. "Yes, that's true."

"That emotion is romantic interest. That's what it feels like when you like someone." She folded her legs into the chair and leaned her elbows on her knees.

"But how, Jazz? How is that possible?"

"How often did you text with him when he was pretending to be an app user?"

"I don't know."

She clutched her hands together and rested her chin on them. "Daily?"

Katrina's lips curved upward against her will. "Many times a day."

"You're feeling the flutter again, aren't you?"

She forced a neutral expression. "Don't be ridiculous."

Jasmine tilted her head.

"Okay, maybe a little. But I shouldn't feel it. He doesn't want me."

"And when you have that thought, it hurts, doesn't it? The ache in your chest grows."

She folded her hands in her lap and lowered her gaze before she whispered, "Yes."

"That's because you like him, and you're afraid the feeling isn't mutual."

"I *know* it isn't."

"Do you?"

Of course she knew. "He never mentioned any flitting and fluttering when we talked."

"Did you mention it to him?"

"Well, no." She huffed. "This is utterly ridiculous for two reasons. One: Succubi aren't capable of love. Two: If we were, then I would be highly disappointed that so much ruckus is created about the emotion. You're telling me love is just some silly fluttering in your belly? There has to be more to it than that."

"Whoa." Jasmine held up her hands. "No one said anything about love. What you're experiencing is *like*. Sometimes like turns into love. Sometimes it turns into friendship or nothing at all."

"Hmph. 'Nothing' sounds about right. He doesn't even want to be friends with benefits. What hot-blooded man passes up an opportunity like that?"

"One who isn't interested in casual sex."

"But all men…"

Jasmine squeezed her eyes shut, her expression pinching before she opened them and spoke, "I wasn't going to tell you this, but Asher and I went to his couples lecture a few days ago."

Katrina gasped. "Traitor!"

"No, babe. Never." She moved to the couch next to her. "It was half out of curiosity and half out of your bestie looking out for you. He doesn't preach celibacy, and from the way he talks, it doesn't sound like he's against sex at all. He teaches people how to connect on an emotional level before bringing physical intimacy into the equation."

Katrina crossed her arms and tapped her foot on the floor. "Your point?"

Jasmine sighed. "When you offered yourself to him, what did you offer? Just your body?"

"Maybe. But that's all I have to offer. What more does he want?" She threw her hands in the air before dropping them into her lap.

"That's not all you have. What about your charming personality and quick wit?"

She arched a brow. "I'm a bitch, Jazz. Everyone says so."

"I disagree." Jasmine patted her knee. "You're my best friend. I wouldn't stick around if you were a bitch to me."

"So, what then? I'm just supposed to be his friend? That's it?"

"It's a good place to start."

"I don't…" Her phone buzzed, and she tugged it from her pocket to find a text from Gabe: *I really am sorry about everything. I hope we can talk soon.*

And there was the flitter-flutter-making-her-want-to-puke sensation. Satan's balls, these emotions were weird.

"You're smiling. It must be Gabe."

She returned her phone to her pocket. "He wants to talk."

Jasmine nodded. "Remember Lucy and Cash?"

Of course she remembered that book. Lucy was a lucky woman. "They were friends in college, and they reunited later in life."

"And friends turned into lovers."

Her throat thickened, and though she tried to swallow the sensation down, it grew until it felt like a lump of dough was lodged at the base of her tongue. "Do they always?"

"No, not always."

And that was the kicker. What if she did become friends with him, and then she liked him even more? What if he didn't like her back? She swallowed again, and the lump seemed to move from her throat to her stomach. She needed to do *something* about these devil-awful sensations, and it looked like becoming friends was her only option.

"It doesn't hurt to try. Thanks, Jazz. You're a good

friend." She portaled into the Bellevue Manor courtyard and stared up at the second-story windows. She would talk to Gabe. She would, but she'd do it on her terms, not because he happened to open his door as she walked past in the hallway. She needed some time alone in her room to gather her thoughts before she faced the man who had made her entire emotional system go haywire.

She couldn't chance taking the stairs in case he was home, but her window stood directly above the patio cover. She'd cracked it when she left for Jasmine's to let in some of the hot and humid air. Gaston kept the place far too cold for a demon's liking.

Stepping back, she eyed the window. The simplest thing to do would be to portal to the patio roof, but she had no idea how far the forcefield extended around the house. If it included the patio, she'd end up flat on her back—not in a fun way—and she'd had enough of that. Her only other option was to climb.

She paced around to the lowest point of the covering and hoisted herself up a beam. Demon strength sure did come in handy. She swung her leg up, catching her foot on the edge of the roof, and pulled herself the rest of the way up.

Bad plan.

Gabe's window stood just to the left of the patio cover, and she caught a glimpse of him inside his room as she crouched on the edge of the roof. He wasn't doing anything spectacular like lying naked in his bed, stroking his one-eyed willy. In fact, he was fully clothed, sitting at the desk and typing on his computer. Yet now, in addition to the fluttering and flitting, her heart beat so hard, it felt like it would burst from her chest. She moved to scramble up the slanted surface, but her legs decided to wobble at that precise time.

She lost her footing and tumbled down, letting out a squeal as she fell to the ground and ended up flat on her back anyway. *Fuck me.*

As she rose onto her elbows, the back door swung open, and none other than Gabe himself came running out. *Double fuck.*

"Are you okay?" He kneeled by her side and took her shoulders in his hands as she sat up. The gesture made her fucking stomach flutter again. If she didn't get this under control, her insides would eventually flutter their way outside, and that would be utterly disgusting.

"I'm fine." She moved to stand, and he helped her up, and damn it…*flutter, flutter, flutter. Fuck!*

He picked something from her hair, and his face held nothing but concern. "What happened? I heard you scream."

Yeah, no. No way in hell was she telling him what really happened. "I portaled too close to the forcefield, I think. It's not the first time it's knocked me on my ass."

Gabe chuckled. "That happened to me once too. Hurt like a bitch."

"No kidding." She smiled, and the tension left her body with the curve of her lips. *What a strange sensation.* "Thanks for coming out to check on me." Her cheeks warmed. Holy hellhounds, she was blushing.

He grinned. "That's what friends are for."

"Are we friends?"

"I'd like to be." He gestured to the chairs on the patio, and she followed him before settling into one.

Flitter, flutter. Jasmine's words rang in her mind. *You like him.* How this was possible, she wasn't sure. She'd never "liked" anyone before. Hell, she could barely tolerate most people, yet something about Gabe drew her in.

Duh. You know what it is, girl. Of course she did. Frankly, she was surprised it took her this long to figure it out. In her entire existence, no one had ever had the strength to tell her no. She was irresistible without any magic at all, but her powers were fail-proof. Well, they had been until Gabe came along. He was the hottest creature she'd ever laid eyes on, *and* he presented as a challenge. Who wouldn't have a tornado in their belly over something like that?

Sure, he was also sweet, smart, and considerate, but those things alone couldn't make a succubus giddy over the prospect of being friends, which could turn into more if she believed the novels she'd read. *Ugh! Now I'm downright confused on top of it all.*

"I think I would like to be friends too, but I have to be honest with you." She held his gaze, chewing the inside of her cheek as she formed the words in her mind. "I'm not sure I know how to be friends." Her breath came out in a rush with her confession. These emotions were getting the better of her. How did people function with the bizarre sensations bouncing around like pinballs inside them all the time?

He chuckled. "I find that hard to believe."

"I'm serious, Gabe. I'm not the kind of person who goes around making friends." Nor did she normally want to. People could be so exhausting.

"Surely you have at least a few."

She gazed up at the afternoon sky. Puffy white clouds dotted the blue canvas, and a heron soared across the treetops on its way to the bayou. The sun warmed her skin, and she closed her eyes for a moment to center herself.

She'd had plenty of conversations with him via text, where she had time to compose her answers perfectly. Talking to him in person made her want to puke, but in an almost pleasant way, if that were possible. She opened her eyes and looked at him. "I have one."

"Okay, then tell me about them. What are they like?" He rested his arm on the wrought iron table, making himself comfortable as if he planned for this to be a long conversation.

Oh, boy. Here we go. "Her name is Jasmine, and she's a necromancer."

He waited a beat for her to continue before asking, "How did you and Jasmine become friends?"

Katrina shrugged. "A mutual disdain for the living?"

He gave her a look that said he wasn't buying what she was selling. "Why do you close yourself off to people?"

"I'm a demon. I'm evil to my core."

"You're not."

"I am."

He shook his head. "Do you want me to list the positive things you do for the citizens of New Orleans?"

If her eyes rolled any harder, she could see her brain. "Why do you insist on finding the good in people? It's like you're almost one of them."

"One of who?"

"The un-evil."

He pressed his lips into a thin line. "I live topside for a reason. So do you."

Well, he had her there, didn't he? She'd grown fond of the topside dwellers over the decades, but it didn't mean she wanted to have slumber parties and tell them all her deepest, darkest secrets. Though, she had done that with Jasmine a time or two.

She blew out a hard breath through her nose. "I met Jasmine when she was a teen. She's the most powerful necromancer in the city, but even the great can have rocky beginnings. A reanimated corpse had gotten away from her in the cemetery. I heard the commotion as she chased it down, and I went in to help her."

"So you've been helping people for *at least* a decade. If that doesn't scream 'evil to your core,' I don't know what does." He grinned and gave her a wink that affected her pulse. How in hell's name did he do that to her with a simple movement of his eyelid?

"Anyway, after I wrangled the body and she removed the ornery spirit, she attached herself to me. She'd never met a demon before, and she talked nonstop for the rest of the night. I found her amusing. She tells dad jokes and makes ghastly puns." She smiled at the memory.

"When did a mildly interesting teenager turn into your only friend?"

"As she grew into adulthood, I began to notice she didn't have friends herself. She got a job at the morgue, and most people—supes included—were either afraid of her power or found her job disgusting. She needed me." She lifted one shoulder dismissively.

"But you don't need her?"

"Well, I suppose I do now. I can't imagine my life without her." She shifted in her seat, the weight of his gaze drawing more words from her lips. "She listens to me, we enjoy each other's company, we're there for each other…"

"So you *do* know how to be friends."

"Not with someone I'm attracted to, someone I like." She clamped her mouth shut. *Holy mother of Cerberus.* She did not mean to say that out loud. Where was a vampire when she needed one? Gaston should offer a free memory wipe on the person of your choosing to every guest because there was no way she could recover from this slip-up.

She stood and wiped her sweaty palms on her jeans. "I just remembered I have a meeting with my app developer. If you'll excuse me." She turned to head for the door, but he caught her hand before she could make her grand escape.

"Katrina, I like you too."

CHAPTER FOURTEEN

"Well, this is an interesting turn of events," Gabe said to his reflection in the bedroom mirror. That was the understatement of the century. What started out as a diabolical plan to win Katrina's heart so he could sabotage her career had made a full one-eighty, and now *he* was the one falling for *her*.

Hopefully they were both falling. Her admission that she was attracted to him came as no surprise. He was an incubus, after all. Everyone was attracted to him. What did surprise him was his impromptu request to take her on a date and then the "yes" that had come from her lips instantly afterward.

Now, he had two hours to plan an epic evening in a city he hardly knew. Thank the Devil for the Haunt Ads. He scoured the site in search of somewhere to take her that would be romantic but also not erotically tempting in any way. Two sex-deprived sex demons together anywhere near an adults-only establishment could be disastrous.

He thought back to her attack on his couples session and the way his inner demon had been drawn out by her power. Yeah, Bourbon Street was out of the question. He needed to find somewhere family friendly.

Scanning the calendar of events, he came across a listing for an outdoor art market two blocks over. It advertised pop-up restaurants, face-painting, and children's games, along with creations from local artists. Sweet Destiny's wasn't too far away, so they could end the evening with a slice of angel food cake to subdue the urges that were sure to surface no matter where they went. "Perfect."

After a quick shower and shave, he dressed in jeans with a dark blue button-up, and he knocked on Katrina's door at seven p.m.

"Be right there," her musical voice sounded from inside. Tonight would be an exercise in self-control for both of them. She was designed to entice sexual attraction, as was he, but he was determined to make things happen on an emotional level. There was too much at stake to fail.

She opened the door, and his breath caught at the sight of her. Dark brown hair flowed in thick waves over her shoulders, and her crimson lips perfectly matched her tight red dress. When she smiled, it reached all the way to her lavender eyes, making his heart throb against his ribs. *Damn.* "You look beautiful."

"When do I not?" She winked and closed her door. "You also look dashing, as usual. The half-rolled sleeves are a nice touch."

"Before we go, can we make a deal? No magic tonight?"

She pursed her lips. "Okay. I can be a good girl for one night, I suppose."

Here's hoping. He motioned for her to head down the stairs first and followed her into the living room.

"If you'll tell me where we're going, I can portal us to the closest secluded spot." She turned toward the back door, but he caught her hand.

"I thought we might walk." He guided her toward the front.

"That's a novel idea." She followed him through the rotating, light-tight door and stepped onto the porch. The early evening sun painted the sky in shades of pink and orange as it began to sink behind the horizon, and he released her hand, shoving his into his pockets before descending the front steps. He had to limit the physical contact no matter how badly his fingers twitched with the urge to touch her.

They walked side by side beneath the towering oaks and crossed the streetcar tracks running down the neutral ground dividing the road. The sound of voices and music grew louder as they approached the festivities.

"I like the sound of this," Katrina purred. "Are we heading to a block party?"

"Not quite." They rounded the corner, and the art market came into view. An inflatable bounce house stood in the center of a small park, and art and food booths lined the sidewalks surrounding it.

"Isn't this…quaint." Katrina tilted her head as if she were confused.

"Not what you were expecting?"

"Well, it isn't dinner and dancing."

He gestured toward a Cajun/Asian fusion pop-up restaurant and then at the people dancing in front of a stage while a Zydeco band played. "It's both."

She laughed, and a beautiful smile brightened her face. "It certainly is."

"My treat this time. What do you want to do first?"

"Hmm…" She strolled into the fray, scanning the options. "That crawfish lo mein looks delicious. Shall we start there?"

He ordered two servings and some sweet tea before finding a picnic table near the stage. Katrina's smile never faded as they ate, and she observed the people around them in wonder.

"I'm not used to the lighter side of the city." She sipped her tea, watching him over the rim of the cup, the look in her eyes making his stomach clench.

"It's all fascinating to me. I can see why so many supes live here."

She set her cup on the table and traced her finger around the rim. "Are you still planning to stay?"

Ah… The dreaded topic. How could they both be successful when their businesses conflicted. It wasn't a subject he wanted to discuss now. Tonight was for forming a bond with the only person who'd piqued his interest in decades.

"I hope to." He stood and gathered their trash before tossing it in a bin. "What do you want to do next?"

A mischievous grin tilted her lips. "I have an idea." She stood, taking his hand, and then guided him toward the bounce house. "I've never been in one of these before. Have you?"

He eyed the blowup contraption that was shaped like a castle, complete with a green dragon sitting atop one of the turrets. Two children slipped out of the net entrance, leaving it empty. "Are you serious?"

"Come on. It'll be fun." She kicked off her shoes and climbed inside. Gabe had no choice but to follow. He couldn't leave the woman to bounce all alone.

She laughed as she jumped, holding her arms out to

her sides, getting higher and higher with each leap. Never in a million years would he have thought someone as poised and self-proclaimed evil as Katrina would let loose and have clean fun. It was the most beautiful sight he'd ever seen.

He jumped with her, his smile so wide it made his cheeks ache. He couldn't remember the last time he'd had this much fun either. They played like children, laughing and throwing themselves against the cushy walls, bouncing off, and barreling toward the opposite side.

They landed on the same inflated section at once, creating a double bounce that buckled his knees. Katrina squealed, pitching forward at the precise moment he toppled. He slammed into her, his forehead smacking hers before they fell. She gasped as he landed on top of her, but he didn't give either of them the chance to act on the opportunity. He shot to his feet and offered her his hand before pulling her up.

"We better let the kids back in." He turned and slid through the opening in the net. Shoes in hand, he paced to a nearby bench as Katrina exited the bounce house.

She slipped on her heels and strutted toward him. "Are you okay? You shot out of there faster than a gluttony demon on his way to a pie-eating contest."

He finished tying his shoe and stood. "I'm good. That smack to the forehead shook me a little, but I'm okay. How about you?"

"I'm also good." She smiled again. "That was fun. This entire evening has been. Thank you."

"It's not over yet. How about dessert?" Beelzebub knew he needed it after being horizontal with her, even if it was only for half a second.

She lifted a shoulder seductively. "Sounds fabulous."

They walked toward Sweet Destiny's, but as they approached the pristine white mansion with blue trim, Katrina hesitated. "This is the angel's bakery."

"Is that not okay?"

"It depends. Are we here because you think I need it? Because I've kept my word and not used an ounce of magic all evening."

"No." He shook his head. "No, that's not why I brought you here at all. I was in the other day, and it was nice and quiet. I thought it would be a good place to sit and talk."

She gave him a skeptical look. "Or are we here because *you* need it?"

After that fall in the bounce house, he most definitely did. "It couldn't hurt, and her strawberry sauce is divine."

They entered the bakery and sat at the same table he'd occupied when he'd come alone. As Destiny entered from the back, her eyes widened.

"Oh! Hello. Umm…" She cut her gaze between them. "Two slices of angel food?"

"With strawberry sauce, please," Katrina said. "I've heard it's heavenly."

"Everything here is." Destiny dished up their cake and disappeared into the back after dropping it at their table.

They ate in silence for a few minutes, and he focused on the calming sensation of the angel magic taming his demon. But when he looked at Katrina, his attraction to her didn't wane. He didn't sense her using her magic, yet the urge to reach across the table and take her hand was undeniable.

Finally, she spoke, "I told you about the only person I've ever cared about, so it's your turn. Tell me about your human."

He closed his eyes for a long blink.

"It's only fair," she said, and she was right. Everything she'd told him about herself so far had made him like her even more. He couldn't expect her to fall for him if he never reciprocated.

"His name was Jason."

When he didn't continue, she asked, "How did it happen?"

"I told you at the HA meeting."

"Not his demise. I mean, how did you fall in love?"

He traced his fork through the sauce on his plate, and his shoulders drew toward his ears. "He was immune to my power."

She laughed, unbelieving. "That's not possible."

"It is, he was, and it fascinated me. Much like how your mild interest in Jasmine bloomed into a friendship, so did my relationship with Jason. But then it turned into more." He shoved a giant bite of cake into his mouth to give him time to think. "I started developing feelings for him I'd never experienced before. We spent more and more time together, until I finally realized I'd fallen in love. He taught me sex wasn't necessary to have a rich, fulfilling relationship, and well… You know the rest."

She set her fork down and smoothed her napkin in her lap. "And that's why you teach your classes. You really believe what you're preaching."

"I do."

Her brow crumpled as she searched his eyes. "I'm really sorry I turned your lecture into a sex-fest."

"You've already apologized, and I've already forgiven you."

"And here we are on a date."

"Here we are." He gazed into her eyes, hoping to hell

she felt the same connection forming between them. Now he understood what Destiny meant when she said he'd lose more than his manhood if he failed. He was falling hard and fast for Katrina Alarie.

They finished their cakes and returned to Bellevue Manor. As they reached the second floor, he walked with her past his room and stopped outside her door. "Thank you for going out with me tonight. I hope we can do it again."

"Me too." She nipped the corner of her lip between her teeth, and his gaze slipped to her mouth.

He shouldn't have looked. She was far too tempting, but he didn't have to wonder what her lips would taste like for long because she rested a hand against his cheek and pressed her mouth to his. They were soft as silk, full and luscious, and when she parted them in an invitation, he couldn't help but slip his tongue between them. *Devil have mercy.* He cupped her face in his hands and drank her in, losing himself to the sweetness of her mouth and her warm, inviting scent.

No! He couldn't do this. She'd made a promise not to use her magic, yet she'd done it anyway. They wouldn't be doing this otherwise; he knew better. He'd never convince her she was capable of love if they succumbed to their demonic natures.

He jerked away. "You swore you wouldn't use your power."

Her mouth fell open in disbelief. "I didn't."

"We can't..." He shook his head, confusion clouding his thoughts. He hadn't felt her magic, had he? No, all he'd felt was desire, so why the hell did he accuse her? His thoughts scrambled, frying like wyvern eggs over hellfire.

"Yeah, well, we did. I kissed you, and you kissed me

back, and I didn't even release a tiny squirt of magic to make it happen. You kissed me because you wanted to." She fished her keycard out of her purse and pressed it against the lock. "I will never understand why people crave these stupid emotions. They make no sense." She disappeared into her room and slammed the door.

CHAPTER FIFTEEN

G abe stood there, drumming his fingers against his thigh and staring at Katrina's door. What the hell just happened? He thought he was making a breakthrough with her, that they were connecting on a deeper level. Then she kissed him, and all he could think about was what her bare skin would feel like beneath his fingertips.

He only had a week and a half left to win her heart, but he wanted her body so badly he could taste his desire. It was like level ten red curry, and licking Katrina from head to toe was the only thing that could tame the heat.

Some fresh air would help clear his head. He turned and bound down the stairs, intent on heading out the front door, but he found Gaston, Jane, Ethan, and two shifters in the sitting room when he reached the ground floor.

"Gabe!" Jane picked up a box and shook it. "We're about to play Cards Against Humanity. Wanna join?"

"No thanks."

She tilted her head. "You look as troubled as an unlucky leprechaun. What's wrong?"

He blew out a hard breath. "Katrina Alarie is what's wrong."

"Uh oh. Did she sabotage another lecture?" She patted Ethan on the leg. "We need to sign up for one of those sessions if that's how they all end up. Don't you think, babe?"

Ethan raised his brow and shook his head.

"No, she hasn't sabotaged anything. I don't..." Gabe lifted his hands and dropped them at his sides.

Jane gestured to an empty chair. "Come on. Tell us about your troubles. Maybe we can help."

"She's a fabulous problem solver," the blonde shifter said. "Hi, I'm Sophie, and this is my husband, Trace."

Why the hell not? He sank into the chair. "I'm Gabe."

"Nice to meet you, man." Trace leaned over and shook his hand.

"He's the one I was telling you about." Sophie smoothed a lock of his auburn hair into place. "Katrina was livid when she found his flyers at the bar."

Trace chuckled, shaking his head. "I would not want to be on that woman's bad side."

"Then mind what you say," Gaston said. "She has a room upstairs."

Sophie pressed her lips together before whispering, "What has she done now?"

"Nothing. She..." *Holy hell.* Did he really want to talk about this with five people he barely knew? Communication was one of the keys to a healthy relationship, and since he couldn't seem to get his head out of his ass and converse with Katrina, he ought to talk to *someone.* "We've become friends. I think we could be more than friends, but she... No, *I* keep screwing up."

Jane laughed. "Are you sure you want that? She's not the friendliest demon on the block."

"You don't know her like I do. She's one of the most caring people I've ever met."

"She's got an interesting way of showing it," Sophie said through tight lips.

"She created Swipe Right because she likes to see people get together. She won't admit she likes helping people, but she does."

"Huh." Jane cocked her head. "So her bitchiness is a façade?"

"It is, and no one takes the time to get to know the person behind the mask."

She screwed her mouth over to the side. "If you say so. What's the problem then?"

"Yeah." Sophie leaned her elbows on her knees. "How do you keep screwing up?"

"I'm not sure…"

They all stared at him, waiting for him to continue.

"We kissed."

More silent staring. They didn't understand the issue, and he couldn't explain the urgency of the problem without negating his contract with Satan.

"We shouldn't have, but we did. Now I don't know what to do about it."

Sophie leaned back and crossed her arms. "Is it true you teach celibacy in your lectures?"

He blinked. "No, not at all. I teach people how to share their hearts and minds, but I don't advocate abstinence. I never have."

Trace furrowed his brow. "Then kissing the woman you like is a problem because…?"

"I want to connect with her emotionally, to build a strong bond before we…"

Gaston let out an exasperated sigh. "Oh, for the sake of the fuck. She is a succubus, my friend."

He rested his hands in his lap. "Which is exactly why being physical with her is a bad idea."

Jane rose and grabbed a bottle of blood from the mini-fridge in the corner before popping it in the microwave that sat on an adjacent shelf. "I can't believe I'm saying this out loud, but the geezer has a point. I don't know what kind of demon you are, but everyone knows what Katrina is. Sex is her first language."

The microwave dinged, and she poured her drink into a glass. "Anyone want anything while I'm up?"

"Bourbon with a splash of O negative, if you don't mind, young one," Gaston said.

"What happened after you kissed?" Sophie asked.

"I pulled away and told her we shouldn't."

She stared at him, widening her eyes like she knew that wasn't the end of the story.

"Then she went into her room and slammed the door in my face."

She grimaced. "Ouch. Way to reject her."

"I didn't reject her."

Jane handed Gaston a glass and returned to her seat on the sofa. "Yeah, you totally did."

His shoulders slumped. They were right. He did. His mind drifted to his time with Jason. It had taken months for him to get over the feeling of rejection when Jason showed no sexual interest in him. Even at the peak of their love, Gabe had craved a physical relationship.

"I don't know Katrina all that well," Sophie said, "but

if you want to show her you care, you have to speak her language."

Jane nodded. "You can't expect a sex demon to form a bond when you won't even kiss her."

Fuck me. He was caught in an endless loop. Katrina needed his body to connect with his soul, but he couldn't give her what she needed until he won her heart…and he couldn't win her heart unless he could give it to her.

Well, asshole. What's your plan now?

"What a crock of hellhound shit." Katrina sat on the loveseat beneath her window, glaring at the romance novel on the end table. Why in hell's name would anyone want to have these emotions swirling in their heart when it was so easy for somebody to come along and squash them?

So much for her plan to have Gabe wrapped around her finger. She didn't know the first thing about having relationships with people. The fact she and Jasmine were still friends was a wonder, so why did she expect to win a man's interest in anything more than sex? Why did she even try? All she had accomplished was unlocking some stupid emotional sensations that had no place in her being. It was time she shoved them back into their box and threw away the key.

First, she'd have to figure out how to mend the fissure Gabe had torn in her heart. The twisting, tightening, agonizing ache in her chest made tears well in her eyes. *Fuck me.* She'd take a thousand lashes with a barbed whip over this pain any day.

A soft knock sounded on her door, but she ignored it. She wasn't in the mood for conversation. Her visitor knocked again, louder this time, and when she still didn't acknowledge the disruption, he spoke.

"Katrina, it's Gabe. Can I come in?"

Why? So he could drive the knife in deeper?

Half a minute passed before he spoke again, "I know you're in there."

She wouldn't be if Gaston hadn't installed his stupid portal stopper. She'd be down on Bourbon Street right now, helping the dancers milk more money out of the men ogling them, but nooo… She was stuck in her damn room.

"I want to apologize for freaking out on you. I…" He sighed. "I'm a relationship coach, but when it comes to my own emotions, I suck. I'm sorry."

Well, wasn't he good at apologies? Still, she couldn't bring herself to open the door. Rejection didn't sit well with a succubus. Hell, it wouldn't sit well with any woman.

His voice sounded closer to the door as he said, "I pulled away when you kissed me, and I shouldn't have. I didn't want to, but I got scared… Anyway, I am sorry for hurting you."

His footsteps retreated, and she shot to her feet and strode to the door. She tugged it open and leaned into the hall. "What did you want to do?"

He turned around, and without another word, he closed the distance between them, wrapped his arms around her, and kissed her.

A flock of hummingbirds took flight in her stomach, flitting up to her chest and making her pulse race. There was nothing she could do—nothing she wanted to do—but kiss him back. His lips were warm and soft, and his body felt good pressed against hers. Her hormones flared, of course. Whose wouldn't in the arms of a smokin' hot incubus? But she felt something *other* as she stood there wrapped in his embrace.

The fact she felt anything at all besides sexual desire was odd as all get-out, but the emotions were too complex for her to ponder now. Instead, she leaned into him, gliding her hands up his biceps, over his shoulders to hold his face.

As the kiss slowed, she leaned back to look into his eyes. "That wasn't so hard, was it?"

"Not hard at all." He cleared his throat.

"Why do you say you suck at your own emotions?"

The skin around his eyes tightened, and he swallowed.

"Do you want to come in? My promise not to use my magic still holds." She stepped aside and gestured for him to enter.

He sat next to her on the small sofa and wiped his hands on his jeans. "Jason was the first person I ever had feelings for. Aside from the normal incubus desires we all have, I haven't been attracted to anyone since. But you…" He angled toward her, his knee resting against hers. "I have feelings for you. Real feelings that I want to explore if you'll give me another chance."

She started to respond but paused. The ache in her chest had returned along with the nauseating swirl in her stomach. *How odd.* The physical sensations of pleasant emotions were the same as for painful ones. The difference lay in how she interpreted them. "Fascinating."

"I know it's hard to believe, but it is possible for—"

"Yes, I know. You make me feel things too." She scooted closer to him. "I want to do things with you— physical things—not for pure primal pleasure but because I like you. Isn't that weird?"

"It's not weird at all." He took her hand.

"Don't get me wrong, the primal pleasure will happen, and it will be mind-blowing, but—"

He crushed his mouth to hers, and Beelzebub have mercy, it was the most passionate kiss she'd ever experienced. *Hot damn.* He leaned into her, laying her back on the couch and sliding his hand up her thigh to lift her dress over her hip. As his pheromones flared, his warm demon scent held a hint of sulfur, making her shiver.

Incubi and Succubi were the only demons who could completely mask their hellish aromas—for obvious reasons. Most humans claimed sulfur smelled like rotten eggs, which couldn't be further from the truth. The scent was nothing short of delicious.

"I smell the hell in you," she whispered against his mouth.

A masculine growl rumbled in his chest. "I smell it in you too. This is what having emotions does to a sex demon."

"Oh my."

He trailed his lips down her neck and nipped at her collarbone before rising to his knees. Not a hint of red flashed in his blue eyes as he removed her panties and tossed them aside. "No magic this time."

Devil have mercy, his gaze was intense. She couldn't even muster the words, so she bit her lip and shook her head.

"I want you, Katrina. Mind *and* body. I'm sorry I made you think otherwise." Lifting her leg, he pressed a kiss to her inner knee before blazing a trail of heat up her thigh. When he reached her sweet spot, she dropped her head back on the arm of the couch and moaned.

All incubi had skilled tongues, but Gabe's prowess hit

an entirely new level. Every movement, sound, and gasp of air she took guided him. He knew exactly what she wanted, the perfect pressure and speed, and the precise time to slide his fingers inside her. It was like he had a direct line into her mind.

Her orgasm coiled in her core, exploding in earth-shattering ecstasy that made her toes curl. Her head spun, and the strange emotions she felt for him settled in her chest, making themselves at home.

He sat up and wiped his mouth with the back of his hand before tugging her dress back into place. His eyes held an unfamiliar expression. No one had ever looked at her like this before, but it made her feel wanted in a way she never knew she'd been missing. *Wow.*

She rose and reached for the top button on his shirt, but he caught her hands and kissed her fingers before lowering them to her lap. "Just you tonight. Let's take it slow."

She laughed. "Surely you don't expect me not to reciprocate after having my mind blown like that."

He tucked her hair behind her ear. "I don't expect anything. I like to give."

"I'm happy to take, but I want to make you feel good." She cocked her head. She wanted him to feel good.

"You find that strange? That you want to do something for me?"

"I do."

"That's why I think we need to take it slow. These feelings we have for each other...I don't want to lose them by falling back into our old ways."

"I don't want to lose them either."

"Good." He wrapped his arms around her, and she rested her head on his shoulder. "Then let's take our time."

CHAPTER SIXTEEN

Let's take our time? Was he insane? Time was the one thing Gabe didn't have. The clock was ticking, and he'd left Katrina's room last night with promises of a slow-burn romance. *Fucking idiot.*

But what else could he have done? Told her the truth? That he wasn't the one man in New Orleans she could fuck without ruining because he'd ruined himself in a bid for his freedom? Sure, that would go over *really* well. Not. He couldn't tell a succubus his bonerschnitzel wouldn't bone. She'd laugh in his face and then send him packing.

He couldn't bear to lose her over something like this. She was far too exquisite to let go. Last night, she'd kept her promise and hadn't used an ounce of her power on him, yet their time together had been nothing short of magical.

His new friends were right. The way to Katrina's heart was to meet her in the middle. By connecting physically, they'd also strengthened their emotional bond, and if he just had some more fucking time...pun intended...he *knew* she would fall in love.

How did he know? Because he was already sliding down that slope, and he planned to catch her at the bottom the moment she fell.

He needed more time, and there was only one person —if you could even call the bastard that—who could give it to him. Cracking open his door, he glanced down the hall and found it empty. He was about to head for the stairs when he heard Katrina's musical voice drifting up from the ground floor. *Damn it.* She'd already gone down for breakfast.

He slipped back into his room and eyed the window. Unless he could reach the patio cover ledge, it would be a straight drop to the courtyard below. Nothing a demon couldn't handle, so he opened the window and climbed onto the ledge.

Trying to move in stealth mode so as not to draw any attention, he lowered one leg and then the other, resting his butt on the sill. As he pushed off, his jeans caught on a protruding nail. He tried to wiggle free, but his hand slipped, and he fell forward, dangling by the literal seat of his pants for a moment before they ripped and he tumbled to the ground.

He landed with a thud, and as he sat up to rub the soreness from his neck, he glimpsed Katrina's wavy hair through the glass on her way to the back door.

Fuck me. He waved his hand, opened a portal, and tumbled through.

The demon entrance to hell was as unwelcoming as ever, with Christmas music blasting so loudly through the speakers, the sound crackled and popped. Hot, sulfurous air pressed in around him, making the trek to Satan's palace feel like swimming through gravy.

Thankfully, the added heat and nightmarish music had

sent the demons running for their homes, and Gabe didn't encounter anyone on his way. He entered the palace and headed straight for the Devil's office. From the corner of his eye, he glimpsed Rosemary, the assistant, shoot to her feet, but as he pushed the door open, she threw her hands in the air and said, "You know what? I give up."

Poor woman. What had she done in life to be tortured for eternity as the Devil's personal assistant? Gabe couldn't imagine.

He marched past the roaring fireplace—oddly, Satan's office was far cooler than the rest of hell—and found the Devil in his high-backed leather chair and a banshee sitting on his desk. She had long, platinum hair that puffed and frizzed like she stuck her finger in a light socket every morning to dry it. Her skin was ghostly pale, and her eyes were such a light shade of blue, they were nearly transparent. She wore a flowing green dress, which meant she didn't work for the Devil. He made all his employees dress in red. She slid off the desk and stood next to Satan, resting a hand on his shoulder as Gabe approached.

The Devil steepled his fingers. "Ah, Gabriel. Has my 'Little Merman' come to admit defeat already? You have another week, don't you?"

The banshee cocked her head. "He's a merman?" Her voice was shrill like a dental drill to Gabe's eardrums. "But he has legs."

Satan closed his eyes, his lids fluttering as if he were rolling them. "It's a metaphor, pookykins. He's tasked with making someone fall in love, but he can't use the one tool that would help the most."

Her face scrunched. "I still don't get how that makes him a merman."

The Devil let out a heavy sigh. "Never mind, Orla."

He pressed a button on his phone. "Rosemary, I need you to bring in my testicle shears and turn the gold smelter on."

"No, Satan." Gabe stepped toward the desk and rested his fingertips on the bone surface. "I need more time."

The Devil laughed, and Orla crossed her arms. "You have enough nuts to feed a swarm of rabid squirrels, my meaty hellflower," she said. "You promised you'd stop collecting balls."

He took her hand and kissed it. "I know, pookykins, and I swear this will be the last time."

"You don't have any space left on the shelf."

"This pair will stay on my desk as a trophy reminder that no one can take Katrina away from me." He clamped his mouth shut, his eyes widening in an *oh, shit* expression that made Gabe chuckle.

"Katrina?" Her voice grew louder and even more shrill. "You say that name in your sleep. 'Katrina, you'll never get away.' I thought she was a tortured soul who tried to escape."

"Yes, pookykins," the Devil pleaded. "You're right. That's all she is."

She stepped away and crossed her arms. "Are you cheating on me?"

The Devil let out a nervous laugh. "No, my sweet Irish pumpkin. I wouldn't dream of it. I haven't seen her in more than a hundred years. I swear on my nut collection."

"That's true," Gabe said, though why he was coming to the bastard's defense, he wasn't sure. "Katrina told me that as well. It's been over a century."

He cut his gaze between the banshee and the Devil. Satan almost cowered in her presence. Maybe he could use this to his advantage.

"I'm trying to make Katrina fall in love with me." He furrowed his brow at Orla, pleading with his eyes. "If I succeed, he has to grant her freedom. She'll be out of your hair for good."

"What's wrong with my hair?" She patted her hands on the frizz.

"Nothing." Gabe sent out a tiny pulse of magic. "It's beautiful."

As a pink blush spread across her cheeks, Satan glared at Gabe. "Do not try to seduce my girlfriend, Gabriel. Your floppycock would only disappoint her."

Gabe's jaw tightened, but he refused to give the Devil the pleasure of knowing his jabs hurt. "Please, Satan. She's coming around, but I need a few more weeks."

The bastard laughed, waving his hand, and a parchment appeared on his desk. "Three weeks, and she has to tell you she loves you out loud. Those are the terms."

He lowered his head, his shoulders lifting and lowering with a defeated sigh before he flicked his gaze to Orla. "I'm falling for her. I know she's falling for me too, but these things take time."

Her lower lip trembled, and her eyes softened in sympathy as she squeezed Satan's shoulder. "Double his time, ghostrider. Give him three more weeks."

Satan waved his hand, making the contract disappear. "Absolutely not. The terms he agreed to stand."

Orla's hand curled, her claws digging into his jacket, her breathing growing shallow as static electricity buzzed in the air around her. "Double his time, Satan."

The Devil straightened his spine and inclined his chin, making him look more like a disobedient child than the Lord of the Underworld. "No."

Orla's hair flowed in an imaginary wind, and her eyes

sparked like a storm brewed inside them. "I said, 'DOUBLE HIS TIIIIIME!'"

A gust of electrified air knocked Gabe back a step, and the fire scorching along the wall was extinguished in a puff of smoke. Even Satan's gelled black hair didn't withstand the scream. Every strand stood on end, and tiny spirals of smoke rose from the tips.

Gabe smoothed his own hair back into place as the Devil made the contract reappear on his desk. He took a pen that looked suspiciously like a boney finger and scribbled on the parchment.

"Anything for you, pookykins." He forced a smile at the banshee before offering the pen to Gabe. "You have three more weeks. Sign here and leave."

Gabe scrawled his name on the revised contract and mouthed the words *thank you* to Orla. Then he turned on his heel and jetted out before the Devil could come to his senses and change his mind.

CHAPTER SEVENTEEN

"It's been almost a month since I've seen you. Are you doing the construction on your house yourself or what?" Jasmine set a glass of whiskey in front of Katrina and sank into a chair at The Tipsy Leprechaun.

It was true Katrina had been neglecting her best and only friend, but she'd been busy. While she wasn't doing the construction herself, she had visited her home several times over the weeks to make sure the rebuild was going as planned. New Orleans had so many rules about keeping things the way they always had been. You couldn't even change your paint color without petitioning the historical society.

She'd had meetings with her app developer to discuss the possibility of more changes to the way people were matched, and she'd been doing…other things.

She ran her finger over the rim of the glass, the flittering fluttering sensation that she'd gotten used to rising from her stomach to her chest. "I've been spending a lot of time with Gabe."

Jasmine laughed. "I can only imagine what an incubus and succubus have been doing together in a B and B."

Katrina sipped her whiskey, focusing on the way it heated her throat down to her belly. The sensation wasn't unlike the way she felt around Gabe—warm and fuzzy. All these physical anomalies that had felt so foreign to her in the beginning now felt…right. It was odd as fuck, but she liked it.

"Would it surprise you if I said we haven't done anything like that since the first time?"

"Uh, yeah. And I'd have to call you a liar after the way you described your first 'encounter.'" She made air quotes. "I know you've been riding the orgasm express daily."

"I would never lie to you, bestie." She smiled and took another sip of her drink. "We are compromising."

"Compromising?" Jasmine arched a brow.

"Believe it or not, this emotional intimacy crap isn't crap after all. We are getting to know each other and forming a bond unlike anything I've ever…" She paused, flicking her gaze to the band as they mounted the stage. "A bond like yours and mine."

"So you're just friends?" Jasmine took a swig of beer as the band played a jazz song.

"No, it's hard to explain. This 'like' that you accused me of in the beginning has grown deeper. I think about him constantly, which, no offense, I do not do about you."

Jasmine leaned her chin on her hand. "You're falling for him."

"I believe I am. I don't know how it's possible, but I am, and I think it's time I showed him how I feel." She nodded in resolve. "Tonight is his last lecture in the series he planned here. When he comes home, it will be his turn to compromise."

"Oh, man. Does Gaston have any more rooms available? I might have to bring Asher there if all that sex magic is going to be flooding the house."

"I promised I wouldn't use my powers on him." And frankly, she wouldn't need to. If he felt half of what she felt for him, tonight would be epic.

"Holy phantom farts. You are falling for him hard."

Gabe adjusted the bouquet of lavender roses in his arm and knocked on Katrina's door. He'd been doing everything demonly possible to win Katrina's heart, but with only three days until the deadline, it was time he pulled out all the stops and proved not only were they meant for each other, but they could be partners as well. It was a flawless plan. So perfect, in fact, he couldn't believe he didn't think of it sooner.

The door swung open, and his body warmed at her beauty. She wore a lavender dress that hugged her curves and matched her eyes, and her hair hung in loose, romantic waves around her shoulders. Her smile brightened her entire face, making his heart thump in his chest.

"How did you know I'd be wearing this dress?" Katrina took the roses and smelled a bloom.

"I got them to match your eyes." He stepped into her room and closed the door. "Before we go out, I was hoping we could talk." He couldn't wait to tell her his idea. Once she heard it, she'd know for certain he was in this for the long haul. And once he proved his love, she'd be sure to say those three little words that would release them both from Satan's control for good.

She laid the flowers on her dresser. "I was hoping we could stay in for a while as well."

He sank onto the loveseat and wiped his clammy palms on his jeans. "Tonight was my last lecture."

"Yes, I know." She laughed and sat next to him, resting a hand on his knee. "Maybe now business will pick back up for me."

"I haven't suggested anyone cancel their accounts like I promised."

"And I added a bio section to my app like you suggested. I think we've gotten good at compromising." She slid her hand higher on his thigh, and his stomach tightened.

He'd convinced her they were compromising by not doing anything sexual since that first time, and she had accepted it in the beginning. But he could tell she wanted…needed…physical touch.

He cupped her cheek in his hand and leaned in to kiss her, but when a soft moan vibrated from her throat, he pulled away. "I've been thinking."

She sighed and leaned her elbow on the back of the couch. "Compromise works both ways, you know."

"I know." And he wished he could give her what she needed. Fuck, how he wanted to give it to her all night long. "Let's talk for a minute first. There's something I want to discuss."

Her brow furrowed with unease. "I hope you're not planning the 'it's not you; it's me' speech."

"No, nothing like that." He grinned. "I have an idea of how we can work together. A way to combine your app with my methods."

She shook her head, confusion pinching her features. "You want to be business partners?"

"It's the perfect setup. You have all the logistics in place; your developer would only need to duplicate what's there and tweak it a little."

She rose and moved to the bed, sitting on the edge of the mattress. "I don't understand. I thought this…"

"We'll have two sides to the app." Excitement made the words tumble from his mouth. "When people register, they can choose which method they want to meet people through. If they're looking for casual hook-ups, they swipe right and see the original program. If they want a relationship, they swipe left and fill out a questionnaire to help us match them based on personality. Swipe Right to Bite, Left for Love. What do you think?"

"I don't…" She wrapped her arms around herself. "I thought… This whole thing…this relationship you've formed with me was all so you could take over my app? So you could steal my livelihood?"

"What?" He rose to his feet. "No, Katrina. That's not it at all."

"Get out." A tear slid from the corner of her eye, and she wiped away. "I want you to leave."

"Sweetheart, listen to me." He moved to sit next to her on the bed, and she stiffened. "I'm not trying to steal anything from you. I want to work together. I want to be partners."

"So you made me have all these…these *feelings* so you could convince me to be your business partner?"

"No." She wasn't understanding. He wasn't explaining it right.

"Yes. Yes, because you knew I would never go for it unless you convinced me all the silly physical sensations meant something. But they don't mean a damn thing, do they? They're used to manipulate and hurt."

"Katrina…"

"I can't believe I let myself fall for this. I knew you were full of hellhound shit the moment I laid eyes on you, but I let myself believe I could… That you could…"

Holy fuck, this conversation wasn't going as planned.

"Is that why you didn't want to be physical with me? Because you're not really attracted to me; you just want my app?" She blew out a hard breath and stood. "I bet going down on me must've been torture for you, wasn't it?"

"I am attracted to you, Katrina. I swear it. I only suggested joining together on the app to show you how perfect we are for each other."

"That's how you show me we're perfect for each other?" she scoffed. "Wow, Gabe. How romantic."

"Listen to me. Listen." He rose, taking her by the shoulders, and she lowered her gaze. "Look at me, please. Look in my eyes."

She lifted her gaze to his, and so much hurt and sadness filled her eyes, he nearly choked on a sob. This was not how tonight was supposed to go. She was supposed to be happy, not devastated.

Satan's balls, he was an idiot. Katrina was a sexual being. She needed physical touch to convey emotion, and he *knew* that. He'd been so caught up in his own needs, speaking only *his* emotional language, he'd completely neglected hers. How the fuck could he expect her to be excited about the prospect of working with him when he hadn't shown her his love was real?

Words wouldn't convince her of anything right now. She needed action, so that was what he'd give her.

"Come here." He wrapped his arms around her and pressed a kiss to her cheek. When she refused to turn toward him, he nuzzled her hair and whispered into her ear, "I'm sorry. You're right; you've been compromising, but I haven't. I've been neglecting your needs."

He kissed her head and pulled back to lift her chin. When she finally looked at him, he kissed her. Soft and tentative at first, his lips lightly brushed hers, giving her ample time to pull back or slap him into next week.

When she rested her hands against his chest, he thought for certain she would push him away. Instead, she leaned into him, deepening the kiss. He closed his eyes, enjoying the warmth of her mouth against his and the feel of her hands gliding around to his back and moving over him, massaging him. He'd have to stop her soon, shifting the attention to her pleasure and not his own, but for now, he basked in her touch.

Katrina was right, going down on her had been torture, but not for the reason she'd thought. The only thing he didn't enjoy about that was his inability to do more.

She slid her hands down to squeeze his ass, and he let her. He couldn't help himself. He wanted her with every fiber of his being, and it was time he showed her. She released his backside, and, before he could stop her, she reached around to squeeze his front.

"You…?" She squeezed again. "You're not hard."

Fuck me. She'd found his secret. His ears burned with embarrassment, and he stepped back, out of her reach. "No, I'm not."

"Is it…" She pressed a hand to her chest. "Never in my life have I questioned my appeal, but you have me wondering for the second time tonight. Is it me?"

"No." He shook his head and looked at the floor. "If

anyone were capable of making me hard, it would be you. Believe me."

"I don't understand."

He blew out a frustrated breath and shoved his hands into his pockets. "It's not you. It's me."

She parked her hands on her hips. "Seriously, Gabe? You can do better than that."

"I haven't had a hard-on in decades." He flicked his gaze to hers, his eyes tightening as he awaited her response.

"You mean you're…impotent?" She crossed her arms, a look of uncertainty drawing her brows together.

He cringed at her use of that word. He wasn't weak or powerless. He just couldn't get it up.

"They make pills for that, you know?"

He laughed dryly. "They don't work." Not that he'd tried them, but he highly doubted a pharmaceutical would negate Satan's magic.

She drummed her fingers on her biceps. "Well, you're in luck."

"Why is that?"

"Because making men hard happens to be my specialty, and I have *never* failed at my job." With a deep inhale, she threw her head back and dropped her soccer mom guise. She hit him with the full force of her magic, and his entire body shuddered in ecstasy. Well, every part of him except the one part that mattered.

She slunk toward him, exuding enough sexual energy to bring the entire cast of Thunder from Downunder *and* the Chippendales to their knees. Invisible fingers danced over his skin, her eyes devouring him as she licked her lips.

He couldn't fight her magic. His own guise slipped, his inner demon coming to the surface and matching her power. A moan reverberated from down the hall, and the headboard in the adjacent room knocked against the wall. Their magic had given every man in the B and B a boner…except for him.

But he didn't care. He took Katrina in his arms and kissed her like his life depended on it. She melted into him, kicking one leg up as he grabbed her thigh and hooking it around his hip. Her hand found his crotch again, and she jerked away.

"You're still not…"

"Doesn't matter." He gripped her hips. "I can make you come all night long." And he planned to enjoy every moment of it.

"It does matter." She reined in her magic and stepped out of his reach. "What's wrong with your dick?"

"I can't pitch a tent, but we're not going camping." He licked his lips, ready to taste every inch of her.

"Why?" She crossed her arms, silently saying their sexy times were through.

Gabe sighed. Of course it mattered. She was a succubus, for fuck's sake. She wouldn't want to be with a man whose dick was as useful as shooting pool with a rope. Damn it. Why did this have to happen now? He was so close…

He reeled in his magic. "I…" His nostrils flared as he forced out a breath. "I traded it to Satan for my freedom."

She laughed, unbelieving. "You did not."

He spread his arms. "How else would you explain it, then?"

"Well, you… I don't know, but no incubus would willingly let Satan turn his man meat into a limp bizkit. Not even for his freedom."

"No? What would you give up for yours?"

She sank onto the bed. "Almost anything, but I don't

know if I'd give up that. You're an incubus. Sex is who you are. How could you surrender your ability to ever have it again? Do you not feel the urges? Can you not be turned on?"

He took a tentative step toward her, and thankfully, she didn't recoil. Ashamed didn't begin to describe the mortification he felt right now. Her questions were valid. She was a sex demon as well, and if she kicked him out and never wanted to see him again, he wouldn't blame her.

But if she loved him…if she would just say the words…he could do the horizontal tango with her until the cows came home.

"I still have the urges, and you turn me on, Katrina. Beelzebub have mercy, do you ever. I accepted the deal shortly after I lost Jason. I didn't think I would ever want to have sex again. I didn't know I would meet you."

"Why didn't you tell me sooner?"

He laughed dryly. "Tell the most beautiful, sensual woman I've ever met that my dick is out of commission? That's not humiliating at all."

She nodded and swallowed hard. "I don't know what to think about all this. First, you lied to me, pretending to be someone else."

"I'm sorry. I thought we were past that."

"Then, all these emotions you've stirred up inside me are perplexing enough, but now you want to be business partners too. Succubi are normally all about mixing business and pleasure, but I can't help but wonder about your motives."

"I swear my motives are pure." Well, they weren't in the beginning, but now they were pure as a virgin.

"I'm so confused. I don't…"

"Katrina…" He dropped to his knees in front of her, taking both her hands in his. "I love you."

Her lips parted, the lower one trembling as her brow scrunched over her eyes. "I…"

C'mon, sweetheart. Say you love me too, and all our problems will be solved. Happily ever after for both of them sat just beyond the horizon. *Two more words…*

"I need some time to think about all this." She tugged from his grasp and stood.

"Katrina…" He rolled to the balls of his feet and rose. "Please…"

"Let me sleep on it, okay? These physical sensations are hard to interpret, and I need some time."

They were nearly out of time. *Satan's balls.* Could he screw this up any worse? Never mind. He didn't want to know the answer to that.

She padded to the door and opened it. "We'll talk tomorrow."

Devil on a doughnut. There was nothing else he could do but nod and walk away.

CHAPTER EIGHTEEN

"Thank you for coming, ladies." Katrina folded her hands on the wrought-iron table. "I know I haven't been the best of friends to you, and I… Well, I am trying to change, and I want to do better."

"No worries, hon," Sophie said. "We weren't exactly civil to you the first time we met, were we, Crim?"

Crimson laughed. "Not exactly. No."

"You know I love you." Jasmine winked, and Katrina smiled.

The canopy of a ginormous oak tree covered most of the B and B courtyard, and afternoon sunlight filtering through the leaves dappled the ground in intricate patterns of light and dark. The sweet scent of magnolias drifted in the air, and a ceiling fan whirring above created a cool breeze on the patio. A streetcar gliding along the track sounded in the distance, and Katrina took a deep breath, attempting to wrangle the thoughts and physical sensations into some semblance of logic.

"Some things have happened to me…between Gabe and me…and I need help making sense of it all."

"We'll do our best," Crimson said.

"What happened?" Jasmine asked.

"He told me he loves me."

Jasmine smiled, but Sophie's eyes widened as if she were in shock, and Crimson's mouth dropped open.

"Oh, come on. Is it really that hard to believe?"

Sophie blinked. "No. No, of course not. How...? How do you feel about him? What did you say?"

That was the problem she needed help with. She didn't know how she felt about him. "I told him I needed to think things through."

"Ouch." Crimson grimaced. "Poor guy."

Katrina groaned. "What was I supposed to say? Feeling things is a new concept for me."

"Do you love him?" Jasmine asked.

"I don't know! I don't know what love feels like. That's why y'all are here. To help me interpret what's going on inside me because I am clueless." She waved her hands around like a madwoman. She *felt* like a madwoman.

"Okay." Jasmine patted her shoulder. "We'll help you figure it out. We already know you like him, right? That was established weeks ago."

"Yes. I like him. I enjoy spending time with him." Who wouldn't? He was sweet, considerate, fun.

"Think about the very first thing you felt when he told you," Sophie said.

"I don't know what I felt. That's the problem."

"She means the physical sensations." Jasmine rested her hand on top of hers and looked at Sophie. "She's still learning to interpret what all the bodily reactions mean."

"Gotcha." Sophie nodded.

Katrina chewed the inside of her cheek and thought back to the moment the words had tumbled from his lips.

Before her brain tried to interpret the sensation—which it sucked at—how did her body react? "My stomach muscles clenched, and my chest got warm. There might have been a bit of nausea, but I can never tell if it's good nausea or bad."

"Was there fluttering?" Jasmine asked.

She smiled. "Lots of fluttering. It felt like a thousand butterflies had just emerged from their cocoons."

"That sounds positive," Crimson said.

"It felt positive until they flitted up past my chest and tried to choke me." She sighed. "I'm past the choking, though, and it feels positive again, but…"

"Uh oh, there's a but. Love shouldn't have buts." Sophie pursed her lips.

"Is it a big but?" Crimson asked. "Buts, and hesitation in general, can be normal in the beginning, as long as they're small buts."

Katrina ground her teeth. She really shouldn't share Gabe's secret with her friends, but she honestly had no clue. If she didn't talk about this, well… She didn't know what she would do. If it helped her figure out what to say to him, he would understand, wouldn't he? If he loved her, he would. And if he didn't, then at least she'd know where they stood.

"I'm going to tell you something, but you have to swear you won't tell a soul. It's so secret you can't even tell your husbands. Do you promise?"

"Well, yeah." Sophie looked at her like she'd suddenly grown horns. "You can't dangle a teabag over our heads like that and then refuse to spill it. We can keep a secret, can't we, girls?"

"Of course," Jasmine agreed, and Crimson nodded.

Katrina let out a slow breath. "I shouldn't. He didn't

even want to share it with me, so if word got around to the rest of the topside demons…"

"Tell you what," Crimson said. "I can cast a spell to make it impossible for us to share your secret."

Jasmine shook her head. "Oh no. You are not casting any kind of binding spell on me."

"It won't bind anything except the secret," Crimson said. "I swear all it will do is make it so if you try to share, the words will get stuck in your throat. You won't be able to speak them unless Katrina says it's okay."

"Come on, Jazz," Sophie said. "It's the only way she's going to tell us."

Katrina nodded. "Yes. Yes, it is the only way I'll share it. He'd be devastated if word got around."

Jasmine gave her the stink eye and turned to Crimson. "Fine. Cast your spell, but you better not screw it up and render us all mute."

"I haven't botched a spell since I got back from hell." Crimson looked each of them in the eyes, and the air thickened around them as she gathered her energy. "Katrina has a secret that isn't ours to share. We accept responsibility. The burden is ours to bear. With this spell, we'll never tell until she deems it fair."

All three of her friends stiffened, and Sophie shivered. "Sometimes I really wish I could do stuff like that. Now, spill the tea, girl. What happened?"

"Gabe is…" She closed her eyes for a long blink. "Let me put it this way. When I imagined falling in love, I expected endless nights of sex. But if I fall in love with Gabe, there will be *no* nights."

"So it's true then?" Sophie rested her arms on the table. "He does advocate celibacy? He won't get naked with you?"

"No, he doesn't." Jasmine furrowed her brow, tilting her head. "I attended one of his workshops, and he doesn't suggest anyone be celibate. What happened, Katrina?"

"He…" She might as well say it. She wasn't going to work her way through these emotions without help. "He traded his dick for his freedom."

"Oh." Crimson's shoulders slumped. "That's a big but."

"How awful." Sophie gave her a sympathetic look.

"It's not that bad." Katrina fisted her hands in her lap, a strange need to defend Gabe igniting in her chest. "He says he's attracted to me, and I know from experience he can get the job done despite his problem. I just can't do anything for him, that's all."

"Have you tried?" Jasmine asked.

"With every ounce of magic I have. I got the whole B and B rocking last night, but our boots were the only ones not knocking."

"Damn," Sophie said. "That really, really sucks."

"Does it, though?" Her knee bounced beneath the table. "I mean, yeah, it would be nice if he could offer the full package, but our relationship is more than sex. We have fun together, I think about him when I'm not with him, he makes me feel all warm and fuzzy inside, which is weird as fuck, but I love the sensation."

Jasmine flashed a knowing smile. "I think you found your answer."

"Oh, my evilness. I think I have." She laughed, half unbelieving and half with so much joy her heart felt like it might burst. "I love him, don't I?"

Crimson nodded. "Sure sounds like it."

"I need to tell him." She stood and stomped her foot. "Crap! I don't know where he is. He left his room this morning, and I haven't seen him since. What if he doesn't show up at the HA meeting tonight? What if he's gone back to San Francisco?"

"We'll help you find him," Sophie said.

"I can scry for him," Crimson said. "Give me just a sec."

Katrina paced in a circle around the table. This was it. She had fallen in love despite Satan's rule. Fuck the Devil. No, she would never fuck him again.

Crimson pulled up a map of New Orleans on her phone, and, resting her hands on the table, she lowered her head and activated her magic. A buzzing sensation filled the air, but it suddenly grew heavy, much heavier and more heated with power than any witch could muster.

Oh, hell. Satan was here.

A portal ripped open beneath the magnolia tree, and fire shot out, singeing the blooms. The smell of burnt flowers assaulted her senses as the Devil stepped through and his gateway slammed shut.

Satan looked hot as hell, as usual, in his deep red suit. His eyes undulated like molten lava, and his dark hair was slicked back perfectly into place. "Katrina, it's so good to see you again."

"What do you want?" She took a step back, and her friends stood and moved to stand by her side. *Wow.* So this was the kind of support you got when you allowed yourself to feel emotions. She should have done this long ago.

Satan laughed and strolled toward her before running his finger along the back of a chair. "It has been brought to my attention that my favorite succubus thinks she's in love."

Good news travels fast. Katrina crossed her arms. "So what if I am? There's nothing you can do about it."

"No, I suppose you're right about that." He rubbed his

thumb across his fingertips before curling his lip and wiping his hand on his pants. "You know I only want what's best for you, don't you, love?"

"Pish. If that were true, you'd have granted my freedom a long time ago. Admit it, Satan. You're jealous because I never felt this way for you."

His gaze flicked to hers, his irises flashing white-hot and his hand curling into a fist. His jaw worked like he was struggling to hold the words inside his mouth, and he turned, gliding down the porch steps to stand in the shade of the oak.

"Truth hurts, doesn't it?" What in Beelzebub's name was she doing? Every demon in her right mind knew backtalking the Devil could land her in the tarpits for eternity...or worse. But she couldn't help herself. Her grudge ran deep.

"Here I came to do you a favor, and this is how you treat me?" He clicked his tongue, chiding her. "I was hoping to offer you a deal, but..." His eyes glinted with his sly smile.

She tried to keep a neutral expression, but her brows lifted against her will. "What kind of deal?"

As he opened his mouth to speak, a giant stream of bird shit fell from the tree, splashing onto his shoulder before splatting across his cheek like he'd been struck with a paintball. Sophie started to giggle until Katrina dug her nails into her friend's arm, stopping her.

Steam shot from the Devil's nose as he peered into the canopy and ignited a fireball in his hand. With a flick of his wrist, he sent it soaring, and the offending bird turned to chicken fricassee, falling to the ground with a *thunk* and filling the air with the savory scent of roasted meat.

"Is it wrong that I'm suddenly craving fried chicken?" Sophie whispered.

"I am too," Crimson replied. "Let's go to Popeye's after this."

Katrina elbowed Crimson. Truth be told, it smelled delicious, but unless her friends wanted to become part of the meal, they needed to zip their lips. "What deal?" she asked again.

Satan tugged the red handkerchief from his breast pocket to wipe his face and shoulder. "A deal to make your business boom." He started to return the soiled cloth to his pocket, but he pulled a disgusted look and dropped it next to the roasted robin.

Katrina narrowed her eyes. Of course he'd piqued her interest. She'd sunk her entire life's savings into her app, and if he could make business boom, she had to hear his offer. But something felt off about this. Her stomach churned in a non-fluttering way, and the sinking sensation in her chest made her heart feel heavy.

Look at that. She'd interpreted her emotions without help this time! Still…it wouldn't hurt to hear the man out, just in case she'd decoded them wrong. "You have my attention."

"Indeed." He chuckled. "I need your help, Katrina. Do this favor for me, and in return, I'll make sure every single supe in New Orleans signs up for your app and doesn't cancel until they find true love…which you and I both know isn't all that and a bag of jalapeño potato chips." He winked, and her skin crawled. Also not a pleasant sensation.

"What favor?"

"I'm training two new incubi whose powers have recently matured, but they simply aren't doing it for me yet." He lifted his brow. "Let me rephrase. They're *doing* plenty for me but not at the level they should be."

"You're training them yourself? I thought your banshee was the jealous type. How's that going?"

"I sent her back to the seventh circle. Her incessant screaming made my head ache, but that's good news for you, love. I'm a free man for the moment, and oh, how I have missed you."

Beelzebub on a biscuit.

"My offer is this. Come to my chambers and help me train the incubi. Teach them all your tricks, and your business will always be profitable. I'll even help you expand to other markets." He winked. "What do you say, love? You never could resist a good four-way, especially with your old flame."

Fuck me. If he had made this offer two months ago, she'd have jumped at the chance—and on Satan and his trainees—to help her business by playing her favorite game. But now, she couldn't muster an ounce of excitement at the prospect.

Her app's success was no longer the thing she wanted most in the world—aside from her freedom, of course. All she wanted was Gabe, and doing this 'favor' would ruin her chance at a happily ever after with him.

"Thanks, but no thanks."

"Oh, Katrina." He clicked his tongue again. "No one can resist the Devil."

She stepped toward him. "I can. In fact, I *have* fallen in love, which is something you could never make me do. You lost this one, Satan. I don't need a damn thing from you."

Blue flames rose in his irises, and the tendons in his neck tightened like guitar strings. Okay, she did need one thing from the Devil. She needed him not to roast her alive for shitting on him like the poor bird.

He forced a laugh. "You pitiful girl. Gabriel has done a number on you, hasn't he?"

She inclined her chin. "He taught me how to love, and he loves me."

"Does he?" He tilted his head, an amused grin lighting on his lips. "Are you certain?"

"Yes. He told me he did."

"Yet you didn't tell him in return." He steepled his fingers in front of his chest.

"I was confused, but I'm not anymore. I was on my way to tell him before you showed up uninvited."

"My apologies for the intrusion, but before you run off to claim your unhappily ever after, there is something you should see." He flicked his wrist, and a rolled-up parchment appeared in his hand. "Remember, I only want what's best for you, love. That's why I'm showing you this." He offered her the scroll.

She snatched it from his hand and carried it to the table, her heart sinking so low she thought it might fall out through her ass. This was a contract. She'd been in Satan's lair plenty of times when he'd made deals, and they were always signed on this thick, yellowing paper. Digital signatures were all the rage nowadays, but the Devil liked the foreboding texture of parchment. He said it fit better with his aesthetic.

Katrina's friends gathered around her as she unrolled the contract, and her gaze immediately went to the bottom of the page to look for the signature.

It was Gabe's.

"Holy spirit spit," Jasmine whispered.

Katrina's throat thickened as she read the deal. Gabe

had promised to make her fall in love with him in exchange for getting his crotch rocket refueled. And he was so sure he could do it, he offered his family jewels in exchange if he failed.

She pressed her hand to her chest as if she could stop the sharp stabbing sensation from tearing her heart in two. "What's…" She cleared her throat. "What's all this say? Some of the lines are blacked out."

Satan waved his hand flippantly. "Redacted information that's not important. Your one true love sold you out. He used you."

"He wouldn't." She read the page again, but it was right in front of her. A binding contract between the man she loved and the Devil. "Ouch. I don't like this feeling at all. Jasmine, how do I make it stop?"

Her friend looked at her with sympathy. "Let's not jump to any conclusions yet. Maybe he has a good reason. Hey, you started out trying to make him fall for you with no intention of feeling anything in return."

"That's true, but…"

"And look at the date." Jasmine pointed to the top right corner. "That was more than a month ago. After everything you've told me, I'm sure he meant it when he said he loved you."

"Did he, though? I don't even know what my own emotions mean. How could I expect to be a good judge of someone else's? Perhaps I was only focusing on the sensations his words made me feel, and I didn't pay attention to the way he said it."

"No, Katrina…" Jasmine picked up the contract, but it disappeared in a puff of smoke.

"You were duped." Satan's voice came from right behind her, and she spun to face him.

"Why would he do this?" It felt like all the butterflies that had made a home in her stomach got sprayed with industrial-strength bug killer and now they were churning in an acidic stew, threatening to spout from her throat like the kid from *The Exorcist*. Graphic and disgusting, yes, but she felt it, nonetheless.

The Devil softened his eyes in faux sympathy. "He's a demon, love. Evil at his core, just like you."

Katrina fumed, and her anger eased the breaking sensation in her chest, so she gave it more fuel. "How dare he?" She fanned the flames. "How dare he come into my town, steal my business, and then try to break my heart?"

And she'd fallen for it. How dare *she?* This was so out of character for Katrina, she didn't even know who she was anymore. She'd allowed herself to become vulnerable, bought into his stupid emotional-intimacy-anyone-can-fall-in-love bullshit.

"How about we get even?" Satan reached toward her, his palm up in an invitation.

"Katrina, don't," Jasmine pleaded, but she ignored her.

"How about we do?" She placed her hand in the Devil's and followed him to hell.

CHAPTER NINETEEN

G abe spent the day away from the B and B, giving Katrina the space she needed to process her emotions. She loved him. He could see it in her eyes, feel it in his bones. He only hoped she would see it herself before his time ran out.

As the sun sank behind the horizon, he stopped by her room in hopes of seeing her before the weekly HA meeting, but she either wasn't there or refused to answer her door. Whichever it was didn't matter. She would have to see him tonight.

Fifteen minutes before the meeting began, he portaled into the alley behind the Priscilla St. James Community Center and walked around to the front of the building. The parking lot sat empty as usual, much like where the San Francisco meetings were held. While the majority of humans didn't know demons walked among them, the foreboding feeling they would get when so many congregated in one place made their self-preservation instincts kick in, and they steered clear.

He arrived early in case there was anything Katrina

wanted to say to him before the meeting began, but as he pushed open the door, he found Mike setting up the chairs in the Circle of Hope. Gabe stepped inside and grabbed a chair from against the wall, unfolding it on his way to the circle.

"I thought Katrina usually set up the meetings." He took another chair and moved it into place. "Is she running late?"

Mike glanced at the door before pacing toward him and clapping his hand on Gabe's shoulder. "She's gone, man."

"Gone where?"

He sighed and sank into a seat, gesturing to the one next to him. "She…" He waited for Gabe to sit before continuing. "She went to hell with Satan."

His mouth dropped open, whatever words he wanted to say not even making it to his throat. Katrina hated Satan. Hell, she'd been hiding from the bastard for a century. She wouldn't willingly go back into his lair, unless…

"Fucking Satan."

"I believe that's her plan."

He snapped his gaze to Mike, and his eyes heated, his inner demon clawing its way to the surface.

Mike fisted his hands on his lap. "I can't tell if the idea enrages you or turns you on, but could you get your demon under control? My wife will kill me if I end up naked without her."

"Sorry." He reeled it in. No matter what a sex demon was feeling, when their power fumed, it always resulted in a room full of horny people. "How do you know she's with Satan? What happened?"

"Crimson was there; I wasn't. She told me Satan

showed up at the B and B just as Katrina was figuring out what her emotions meant. He claimed you were manipulating her, that if you could get her to fall in love, Satan would return your…the price you paid for your freedom."

His jaw clenched. "Did the bastard tell them what the price was?"

"He did." Mike grimaced. "I can't imagine losing my…but I get why you'd want it back. Not sure Katrina would have been the one I messed with, though."

His heart sank, his stomach turning into a churning mess of sourness. "And she believed him just like that?"

"He showed her your contract."

"Then she also knows if she falls in love, she'll gain her freedom as well."

Mike shook his head. "Crimson didn't mention that, though she did say there were some blacked-out parts that Satan said were redacted."

"Fucking pitchfork-wielding wannabe Bond villain." He shot to his feet. "Why did she go with him?"

"She's hurt, man. Your plan worked. She loves you, but Satan stopped her from telling you. He offered to force every supe in New Orleans to join her app if she'd go to his palace and have a four-way with him and two new incubi."

No. He couldn't let that happen. If she let her demon take control, with that many people for that long, he'd never get her back. All the work he'd done chipping away the walls around her heart would be for nothing.

"I have to stop her." He waved his hand, opened a portal, and darted into hell.

Ominous silence engulfed him as he made his way from the demon entrance, down the rocky path toward the palace. He almost preferred the Christmas music over this deafening quiet, and as he passed the line for general soul processing, it seemed the dead preferred it too. They stood in line, clutching their hands over their ears and wailing as if the lack of noise was torture.

Fucking Satan. Of course it was. The Devil was about to win the rest of Gabe's manhood, so he was spreading his own morbid form of joy throughout hell.

Gabe growled and stomped across the bridge. He should have known Satan would cheat. Katrina was his favorite succubus, and she had rejected him. He'd held on to the resentment for more than a century. He wasn't going to let her go so easily. The prick probably thought doing her a favor after all these years would soften her up to him. That since she was now capable of love, she would finally fall for him.

"Over my dead body." And demons couldn't die, so there was no way in hell the Devil was taking Katrina from him.

Katrina eyed the two naked incubi lying in Satan's bed. Their bodies were perfectly sculpted, of course, with rippling abs, strong arms, and ginormous dicks. They kissed, and as they stroked each other's cocks, Katrina did feel a slight tingle in her own nether region…but not enough to make her want to strip and join them. *How odd.*

The Devil took off his jacket and laid it on a chair. "Before we get started, love, there's the matter of the contract." He flicked his wrist, and a parchment appeared in his hand. "You join me in teaching these two all your tricks—which could take days if we're lucky—and when we're done, you'll be free to return topside or stay here if you so choose."

"Why would I want to stay here?"

Satan shrugged and grabbed a pen from a bookshelf. "You can come and go as you please. The banishment will be lifted."

She crossed her arms and returned her gaze to the men in the bed. She should have been excited about this. Guaranteed career success for a days-long four-way with three hotties… It was a no-brainer. It *should* have been a no-brainer, but something gave her pause. A tugging sensation in both her head and her chest reminded her of the nagging feelings the heroines in the romance novels would get when they were about to make a stupid decision.

Was this her black moment? The point from which there could be no coming back? She sucked in a sharp breath. That was exactly what this was. If she did this…if she signed Satan's contract and had a sex-fest with these guys, she would never have to worry about her business again.

But what good was her career when the man she loved didn't love her in return?

Maybe it was all a big misunderstanding. Those things happened way more than they should in novels, so why not in real life too? What if Gabe had made the deal with the Devil because he was already in love with Katrina? Making her fall in love with him would have been his goal, whether he was getting anything from Satan in return or not. And getting the use of his danger noodle back would benefit them both.

She crossed her arms. How cocky of him to be so sure he could win her heart that he'd wager his cajones, though.

No, he was after something else when he signed that contract. Something he wanted more than to fall in love.

"Do you need to visit the little girls' room before we begin?" Satan laid his shirt on the chair with his jacket. Damn, that man had a wicked bod, which he obviously thought would get her to sign the contract floating in front of him as he undressed. "You look like you need to make an offering to the porcelain throne."

She pinched her expression even more. "I do not need to poo. I'm thinking."

"It's not a good look on you." He unzipped his pants and let them drop to his ankles. Thankfully, he hadn't gone commando like he used to. Instead, he wore glittery red briefs with horns on either side of his package and a pair of googly eyes right on the bulge. "Let us take your mind off whatever it is that's making you look like your greasy dinner has gotten the better of you. Come, Katrina. Sign the contract."

"Hold on. I'm having a moment here." A moment of utter confusion, to be honest, but a moment, nonetheless. Or maybe it was clarity… "Let me see Gabe's contract again."

Satan waved his hand, making her parchment disappear. "The deal he made is of no concern. He deceived you. That should be enough to make you want revenge. If everyone is on your app, no one will need his cheesy emotion classes." He stepped out of his pants and laid them neatly on the chair.

Two-months-ago-Katrina absolutely would have wanted revenge. Today-Katrina wasn't sure what she wanted.

"Tell you what, love. If you don't want to sign the

contract, that's fine. You are still welcome to join the three of us. Or just me if you prefer a little one on one action."

"If I do this, and I have misread Gabe's intentions with his contract, any chance I had at finding happiness with him will be ruined." And that was what she wanted, wasn't it? To live happily ever after with Gabe.

"Nonsense." The Devil waved his hand like he thought she was an idiot, which was something he did often back in the day. It was no wonder she never felt anything more than physical attraction to the arrogant bastard. "Don't be stupid, love. Gabe can never give you what you need. His flaccid flopper is useless, so even if you did get back together, he would understand. He'd want you to be happy."

She ground her teeth. Stupid she was not. "Why now?"

"Why now what?"

"It's been more than a hundred years. Why do you suddenly want me now?"

"I told you, love. I'm between girlfriends."

"No." She shook her head, backing away. "Let me see Gabe's contract. How much time did he have left?"

Satan let out a nervous laugh. "It doesn't matter. Look at all this man meat waiting for you to devour it." He gestured to his cock and then to the incubi writhing in the bed.

"I don't want your tube steak or theirs. I love Gabe, and whether he loves me back or not, it doesn't change the way I feel."

"But you're hurt."

"And? Being hurt doesn't mean I have to revert to my old ways and do your bidding. I'm leaving."

"You can't leave yet, Katrina." He flicked his gaze to

the incubi before jerking his head toward her. The men crawled out of the bed and slunk toward her like predators, their eyes glowing red, their magic on full blast.

Uh oh. This wasn't good. Her body responded, her own power flaring to life for a hot minute. But the moment she pictured Gabe's face, his sweet smile and kind eyes, she was able to reel it in and maintain control. She would not be playing with Satan's balls or the flesh sabers that were moving toward her.

"Two days, love," the Devil purred. "Then you're free to go."

Her heart raced, and she backed toward the door. "You can't keep me here."

"Indeed, I can." His eyes pulsed like glowing coals. "I own you, remember?"

"The hell you do," Gabe's deep, velvety voice sounded from behind her, and she spun to face him.

"Gabe." Her lower lip trembled, and she took a step toward him. Then she stopped, all the confusion returning in a swirling, sickening tornado of so many emotions she wouldn't be able to name them all if she were born human.

"How did you know where to find us?" Satan growled, and the incubi retreated to his sides.

"I used to belong to you too."

"Mmm..." The Devil licked his lips. "Yes, you did. How about you join the four of us for old time's sake? I'll make your dick work for an hour or two dozen..."

Gabe ignored Satan and strode toward her. "Katrina..." He took her gently by the shoulders. "I meant it when I said I love you. Please don't do this."

"But..." Tears gathered on her lower lids as she whispered, "I saw the contract."

He sighed heavily. "You didn't see the whole thing."

Her throat thickened, and she fought the urge to wrap her arms around him. "Some parts were redacted."

"Because he didn't want you to know." He cupped her face in his hands and wiped a stray tear from her cheek.

"Go ahead and tell her." Satan sauntered toward them, his voice taking on a mocking tone. "Tell her what it says so we can end this game."

"What does it say, Gabe?" she forced the words over the lump in her throat.

"I can't tell you. If I do, he wins."

"I don't…" She jerked from his grasp. "How can I trust you if you won't tell me what it says? You wagered my heart for your dick."

"I did, and I'm sorry for that. I let my pride get in the way of my decision, but in my defense, you had just sabotaged my lecture."

"And I apologized for that!" Her nails cut into her palms as her fists tightened. "If we're going to be digging up our mistakes from the past, well, that's not a fair fight."

"I don't want to fight."

"I want you to." Satan adjusted his dick through his undies. "This is hot."

"Please." Gabe took her hands, uncurling her fists. "Forget about the past. Right now is all that matters, and right now, forevermore, I love you. We had a rocky start, but I wouldn't trade it for anything. You are all I want."

She swallowed the thickness from her throat, and the butterflies returned to life in her belly. "We're like enemies to lovers."

He chuckled. "That's exactly what we are."

"All right. That's enough." Satan flicked his wrists, driving them apart with a pulse of power. Katrina slid backward, and as her legs met the edge of the bed, she fell onto the mattress.

She struggled against Satan's hold, and when she finally sat up, she found Gabe hovering in the air, an invisible hand gripping his throat so hard his eyes bulged from their sockets.

"Let him go!" She scrambled to her feet and clutched the Devil's extended arm, but her strength was no match for his. "Please, Satan. Don't hurt him."

The Devil looked at her like she was crazy. "I'm the Prince of Hell. Hurting people is what I do." His grip tightened, and Gabe let out a pained wheeze.

Katrina dropped to her knees. "I'm so sorry, Gabe. I love you!"

"Fuck!" Satan threw him against the wall and stomped his foot. "You weren't supposed to say that. Now you've ruined everything!"

Gabe slid to the ground, and Katrina crawled to his side and laid her palm on his chest. "Are you okay? Oh, please be okay. I don't want to live without you."

"Do you mean that?" He gripped her hand.

"Fuck, yes. I love you, Gabe. I didn't think it was possible, but I do. One hundred percent."

"In that case, I'm better than okay." He slid her hand down to his crotch, where she got a palmful of rock-hard cock.

Her lips parted on a gasp. "It worked."

"Yes, it did. I love you too."

"Nooooo!" Satan wailed and dropped to his knees dramatically, shaking his fists at the ceiling like a bad actor in an even worse one-man show. "This can't be! You can't have her!"

Gabe's contract appeared in the Devil's hands, and his

eyes darted back and forth as he read and reread the page. "There has to be an out. I *know* I gave myself an out."

"Sorry, Satan." Gabe rose to his feet, tugging Katrina up with him. "The Devil never reneges on a contract."

"I don't, but I would never allow you to take her. It's in here somewhere." He held his forked tongue between his teeth, his grip tightening on the parchment until the edges crumpled. "I won't lose her."

"Take who?" Katrina clutched Gabe's bicep. "He won't lose who?"

Gabe looked into her eyes, and something in her chest snapped. A rush of cool...what was this? Excitement? Relief? She wasn't sure, but it flowed through her veins, making her legs tremble.

He smiled, and his blue eyes sparkled with love. "You, Katrina. He lost you."

CHAPTER TWENTY

"I'm...free?" Katrina's mouth hung open, and the look of surprise on her face was the most adorable thing Gabe had ever seen. "You bargained for my freedom?"

He cupped her face in his hand, running his thumb over her cheek. "That was the part Satan blacked out on the contract. The part I couldn't let you know about or he would win."

She laughed, shaking her head in disbelief. "But, why? You hated me when you made the deal. We were enemies."

"I never hated you. When I heard your story about how Satan refused to cut you a deal, I thought if I could make one for you, it might soften you up, make you like me." He shrugged. "I'll admit in the beginning my motives were business-related, but the more I got to know you...I fell in love with you."

"Motives aside, that's the nicest thing anyone has ever done for me." She kissed his cheek. "Thank you."

"You're very welcome. Let's get out of here."

"No!" Satan stood in front of the door. "If love is what you want, look at me. I've loved you for centuries."

Katrina shook her head. "No, you don't love me. You're obsessed with me because I'm the only person to turn down your offer of moving into the palace. Rejection hurts."

The Devil shrugged one shoulder. "Love. Obsession. It's the same thing."

"It's not, though," she said, "and I hope one day you'll learn the difference."

He narrowed his eyes and stepped away from the door. "I didn't think you'd pull it off, Gabriel, but you got lucky. Both of you. Congratulations."

Gabe opened the door, and Katrina paused in the threshold, turning to Satan. "You could benefit from attending one of Gabe's lectures. Or at least read a romance novel or two."

They left Satan standing there in his sparkly Devil-horned briefs and made their way to the demon exit. As they stopped in the rocky cavern and prepared to portal, Gabe took a long, deep breath. "Beelzebub willing, this is the last time we'll have to smell this much sulfur."

Katrina rested her hands on his shoulders. "Don't forget the weekly Hellions meetings. Those guys can't hide their scent like we can."

He laughed. "Yeah, but it's nowhere near this bad. Goodbye, hell."

"Hello, happily ever after."

"Speaking of happy." He gripped her hips, tugging her toward him. "I've got a little demon in my pants who would love to come out and play."

She leaned into him, sliding her hand between their bodies to grip his cock through his jeans. "There's nothing little about him."

He closed his eyes, the sensation sending an electrical

jolt from his groin to his toes. "Holy fuck, that feels good."

"Take me home."

"With pleasure." He opened a portal and pulled her through. As they landed in the Bellevue Manor courtyard, he took her hand, and they practically ran inside. It had been decades since he'd had a hard-on, and he could not wait to use it.

They reached the living room and found Gaston sitting on the sofa with a tall, curvy blonde. The vampire arched a brow as Katrina tugged Gabe up the stairs.

"It might be a good night to stay in." Gabe winked at him and followed Katrina to the second floor.

"Your place or mine?" She palmed his cock again, making his entire body shudder.

"We can do it right here in the hallway if you want. I need you, Katrina. Right now."

Her musical laugh danced in his ears as she unlocked her room and pushed him inside. "No magic." She tugged his shirt over his head and tossed it on the dresser. "I want to experience *all* the feels when we do this."

"I'm not sure I'll be able to hold it in. It's been a minute for me."

"Try." She took off her shirt and unhooked her bra, letting it fall to the floor.

"Fuck, you're gorgeous."

"That's a given. Tell me why you love me." She wrapped her arms around him and licked his ear, nipping his lobe and raising goosebumps on his neck.

The skin-on-skin contact made his knees feel like jelly, and he leaned against the wall, brushing his lips to her ear. "You're smart and funny." He licked her neck, trailing kisses down to her shoulder.

"Mmm…" The erotic sound made him shiver as she unzipped his jeans and shoved them to the floor. "Tell me more," she whispered.

"You're strong and capable. You run a successful business, which is hot as sin, and you care about people, even though you try to hide it."

She leaned back and let out a long, slow breath. "You have no idea the kinds of emotions that are swirling around inside me. I can't even begin to describe them."

He chuckled and unbuttoned her pants. "Oh, I think I have a pretty good idea."

Her smile brightened her lavender eyes as she worked her jeans over her hips and kicked them aside. He toed off his shoes and removed his pants, his dick straining against the fabric of his underwear. When her gaze dropped to his groin and she licked her lips, he couldn't hold back anymore. He took her in his arms and crushed his mouth to hers.

Beelzebub have mercy, she felt divine in his embrace. Her skin was as smooth as silk, warm, and decadent. Her lips were soft, and her kiss packed so much heat he thought he might spontaneously combust.

He held her tight to his body and guided her to the bed. They fell to the mattress together, a tangle of limbs and pounding hearts, and he drank her in, running his hands over her curves, memorizing the way she felt in his embrace.

Slipping his thumb into the band of her lacey black panties, he pushed them down her hip. She wiggled out of them, tossing them aside before rising onto her knees and yanking his underwear down. With a wicked grin, she took his cock in her hand and stroked it. The sensation of her soft fingers wrapped around him, squeezing him, made his balls tighten, and every nerve ending in his body flared to life.

"I have been wanting to do this to you for weeks." She lowered her head and licked him from base to tip, and Devil damn it, he lost control.

He fisted the sheets and moaned, his demon rising to the surface and sending out a pulse of magic as he splooged all over his stomach. Katrina sat up, and the sound of doors slamming and headboards knocking echoed from the halls.

"Holy fuck. I'm sorry." His ears burned with embarrassment, and he reeled his magic back in. Some incubus he was, coming with the first swipe of her tongue.

"I guess we know how many licks it takes to get to the center of your tootsie pop." Her brow furrowed. "Are you always a quick draw?"

He squeezed his eyes shut. "Cut me some slack. It's been decades, and you are the most beautiful, sexy, come-worthy creature I have ever been with."

She smiled sympathetically. "I'm sure it will be better next time, after you recover."

"After?" He pushed to a sitting position and kissed her. "I think you're forgetting what I am. Incubi don't need to recover." He flipped her onto her back, and she gasped, the wickedness returning to her smile.

"No magic," he said.

She shook her head. "It's just me and you."

Gripping his cock in his hand, he teased her hot folds, slipping his tip inside before circling it over her clit. Her erotic moan melted in his ears like fine chocolate, and as her fingers dug into his skin, he pushed inside her, filling her completely.

"Oh, Gabe!" she cried out and wrapped her legs

around his waist, taking him even deeper. She threw her head back as he pumped his hips, squeezing her eyes shut before opening them and holding his gaze.

Her expression held so much emotion, he couldn't have looked away if he tried. Not that he wanted to. She was exquisite in every way.

"I love you, Katrina."

"Oh, my wickedness, I love you too. Harder, Gabe. Harder!"

He was happy to obey. He slammed into her, burying his bone to the hilt, over and over until her nails dug into his back, and she screamed. Her entire body shuddered with her orgasm, and he joined her, wrapping his arms beneath her and nuzzling into her neck as he came again.

"Holy fuck, that was amazing," he panted against her ear, and she circled her arms around him, holding him like she was afraid to let him go.

He lay there on top of her, basking in the afterglow, but when she didn't loosen her grip, he lifted his head. "Hey. What's wrong."

"Nothing." She held him tighter. "I feel wonderful, but…"

"But?" He pulled away to look at her, and she finally released her hold.

"There are just so many emotions. It's going to take me a while to get used to feeling so much."

He ran his fingers across her forehead and down her cheek before pressing his lips to hers. "I'll be here with you every step of the way."

She nodded, and he rolled to his back before pulling her to his side. She lay her head on his shoulder, and he could feel her smile. "My house should be ready next week. If you're tired of Hotel Transylvania, you're welcome to stay with me."

"I am yours forever."

"And I like your idea about making *my* app *our* app. I think we'll be a good team. I even like what you called it."

"Swipe Right to Bite, Left for Love?"

She ran a finger across his chest. "I'll swipe left on you all day long."

ALSO BY CARRIE PULKINEN

Haunted Ever After Series

Love at First Haunt

Second Chance Spirit

Third Time's a Ghost

Stand Alone Books

Sign Steal Deliver

Flipping the Bird

The Rest of Forever

Bewitching the Vampire

Soul Catchers

ABOUT THE AUTHOR

Carrie Pulkinen is a paranormal romance author who has always been fascinated with things that go bump in the night. Of course, when you grow up next door to a cemetery, the dead (and the undead) are hard to ignore. Pair that with her passion for writing and her love of a good happily-ever-after, and becoming a paranormal romance author seems like the only logical career choice.

Before she decided to turn her love of the written word into a career, Carrie spent the first part of her professional life as a high school journalism and yearbook teacher. She loves good chocolate and bad puns, and in her free time, she likes to read, drink wine, and travel with her family.

Connect with Carrie online:
www.CarriePulkinen.com

Printed in Great Britain
by Amazon